CUBOP CITY
BLUES

CUBOP CITY
BLUES

PABLO MEDINA

Grove Press
New York

Published simultaneously in Canada
Printed in the United States of America

FIRST EDITION

ISBN-13: 978-0-8021-1984-1

Grove Press
an imprint of Grove/Atlantic, Inc.
841 Broadway
New York, NY 10003

Distributed by Publishers Group West

www.groveatlantic.com

12 13 14 15   10 9 8 7 6 5 4 3 2 1

For Arístides Falcón Paradi

Le monde bat de l'autre côté de ma porte.
—Pierre Albert Birot

He vivido en el monstruo y le conozco las entrañas.
—José Martí

Beat on those tom-toms, man.
—Dizzy Gillespie to Chano Pozo

CUBOP CITY
BLUES

STORYTELLER

I came to Cubop City as a boy, brought here by my parents, who fled one Sodom and entered another and never looked back. My father was a soap maker, my mother was a housewife. Before I was born, she'd been an aspiring torch singer. After I was born she gave up the torch and tried to be a mother but motherhood wasn't in her. She did everything in her power to keep me from coming into being, but she failed. Here I am.

Growing up I heard her singing in the shower, her voice silky and seductive. Dry, she wrung her hands and became ill—moans and wails coming out of the bedroom. A burning in her womb. My grandmother took care of me, my grandmother who was all power and love, bountiful love and meaning, and when she could no longer, a bevy of aunts fawned over me.

There was Leonora, who bathed and dressed me; Alba, who woke me and powdered me with talcum; Minerva, who tried to teach me the ways of the world; and Carlota de Los Ángeles, who made me kiss the Virgin every day, though I never learned what that brought or why it was better than eating a banana or listening to rain splattering on the roof. Finally, there was Marina, who took me to the beach and told me that all great things come from depth. She put wreaths of seaweed on my head and made me stand at the water's edge so that I could feel the tongue of the sea at my feet. I couldn't take a step without their knowing; I couldn't say a word without their leaping with excitement in exultant dances, quick flighty steps into the light of the future. I woke up at night clawing at the mosquito net, thinking my mother's illness was my fault. Years later, I found out it was.

In Cubop City, my father became a teacher of high school Spanish, my mother a secretary for a perfume magnate. In reality she was his mistress. Her womb stopped burning. She brought home perfumes, leftovers from the magnate, and the apartment smelled of My Sin.

My father accepted his horns with convenient indifference. By the age of twelve, when I began to feel the pull of sex, I suspected that he was having an affair with Cornelia, the housekeeper. I heard them giggling in the kitchen when they thought I was asleep in my room, and there was something in his tone of voice when he spoke to her that wasn't there when he spoke to my mother—complicity, duplicity, the quicksilver language of love. Mama and Papa never fought, but between them was a space I filled and cushioned, like cartilage between two bones.

Cubop City was subject to its own rigors and laxities and demands and dynamics. Gone were my grandmother and my aunts, gone the slow warm days of the tropics, the creatures Minerva brought me—slugs, toads, and lizards she dissected so I would learn how the world worked. The answer's in their entrails, she said. She'd pull out the lungs, the stomach, and the liver, and lay them out on wax paper. There, she said. Where? I asked, moving closer. All I saw were tiny lumps of tissue, wet and spongy to the touch.

In Cubop City I heard the steam shovels digging, the workmen screaming orders at one another, the taxis and trucks blaring out their songs like maladapted geese. ¡Ey, Papo! ¡Ey, Mamita! Coming through, coming through. Get that van out of here. I'm making a delivery, man. Move that piece of shit or I'll give you a fucking ticket. Cock-sucking scumbag pig.

Mama, what is a scumbag?

What your father wasn't wearing the night you were conceived, she might have said but didn't, as my father wasn't really my father. Instead, she answered, Nothing, an insult. You shouldn't repeat it.

I was born nearly blind, couldn't see but six inches in front of my face, sometimes seven or eight if I'd rested sufficiently the night before. Beyond that was a gray ooze filled with indistinguishable forms, emanations from the bodies of those close to me. When I reached out and touched them they were solid and responded in the ways those close to you respond, affectionately, patiently. Then I'd move in close enough to make out their features—my father's Roman nose, my mother's stony eyes, the smudge of her mouth, the dry riverbeds of her hands. When their patience wore out, they spoke. ¡Ay, muchacho! Enough. Go read your encyclopedia.

For I was, if nothing else, an avid reader of the Britannica, 1911 edition. It was one of the first things my parents bought in our exile to replace the one we'd left behind. I hovered over the tomes like a dirigible. The day my father found me reading volume 1 was a great moment for him. It's a miracle! he said. My mother, or the shadow I imagined was my mother, stood beside him and looked down at me. I felt then the canyon of shame and guilt between us. What was the source? Love comes in many guises.

Of course it was not a miracle. I'd simply convinced the housekeeper to teach me to read English as she had taught me to cook. All men, even nearly blind ones like you, she said, should know how to prepare a few dishes. I learned more than a few. Cornelia was Hungarian by birth and had been a university professor on the island. She had a degree in philosophy from the University of Frankfurt, but in Cubop City her degree counted for nothing. As I said, she was hired to care for me and to cook and clean. Her affair was with Papa. I heard her frolicking in the kitchen, laughing the way Europeans laugh, a prelude to pleasure.

I'd learned enough to identify words in English. Pronunciation was another matter. Out loud, things came out sounding like a Finno-Ugric version of Old English. My father insisted I was a genius. I was remaking the language. From then on he was at my disposal, especially in matters of the mind, and provided me with all the books, magazines, and documents I requested, and many I didn't request but he felt compelled to place strategically in my room: mathematical and scientific treatises, studies by famous linguists and philosophers, things I didn't understand and had no interest in. As I said, I was not a genius, just a boy with a lot of time and a curiosity of the world beyond the six inches in front of his face. Study at your own pace, he said. Read what you want. And I did, filling the house with dictionaries, manuals, picture books of all sorts, comics, and graphic novels about Mexican wrestlers and Cuban boxers, my face floating over the varied topography of the texts as all else receded into a milky snowfield like an infinite margin, a wall-less labyrinth where all limits fell away.

Grey's Anatomy I asked for and Grey's Anatomy I got, as well as large-print editions of *The Origin of Species, The World We Live In, Moby Dick, The Double Helix, Don Quixote (with illustrations by Doré), The Mysterious Island, The Tigers of Mompracem, Two Years Before the Mast, Adventures of Huckleberry Finn, The Count of Monte Cristo, The Four Horsemen of the Apocalypse, The Art of Bullfighting, The True History of the Conquest of New Spain,* and *The Knights of the Round Table* illustrated by N. C. Wyeth. It was only when I asked for a copy of the Bible that my father responded with a definitive no, his inbred anticlerical fervor rising to the surface like a thick black poison. I'll not have a priest lover in my house. Hijos de la gran puerca!

On the chance that I was a genius, he put aside his prejudice and found, in a used bookstore downtown—where there used to be many and now there are few—a battered King

James version of the Bible dating to 1865, which elevated my young and burgeoning English to tolerable heights. The text was crammed and small, and the reading was arduous, but I loved the feel and smell of the old pages and the pressed flowers and bits of paper on which were scribbled notes about the weather, the harvest, the bread making. Then, in between the pages of Matthew, I found a treasure. It was a letter from a Skene Gordon in Alicedale, South Africa, to his mother. It was dated 1883.

> *My Dear Mother, I suppose you are angry with me for not writing, but I have been very ill since I left and I am sorry to say I am not much better—You must excuse me, writing a long letter as I am still very unwell and am scarcely able to get to do my work However I am very glad to say that I am getting better, but very slowly The baby has been christened since I came out and her name is Mary Skene Gordon I have nothing more to say except that I am anxious to know how father and everyone else are in health You ought to have written by now You Affect. Son, Skene.*

I was beyond myself with excitement. The Biblical text left me cold. The letter, though, was alive—not because of what it said but because of what it didn't. I found the Britannica map of South Africa in volume 25 and located, after a long time of hovering over it, the town of Alicedale, northeast of Port Elizabeth. I read the letter several times and tried to build a world around Skene. Was he angry, contrite? I didn't know what anger was, or contriteness or joy or fear. To me all emotions were the same—beans in the soup, kernels in the labyrinth, tufts of grass growing out of the frozen flatlands of the spirit, if spirit there was. I found things out eventually, as one is prone to do. The Hindenburg burning is not a metaphor for passion. A stormy sea is not a metaphor for passion. Or a thunderstorm. Or an earthquake. A lamb suckling her mother is. A worm slithering on the ground. Grass growing at the foot of the cross where Christ is hanging. A mirror without reflection. There was no joy in Alicedale. *You ought to have written before now.* Was Skene chastising or speculating? And that abbreviation in the closing—was he simply too busy or sick to write out the full word, too reticent to give his mother the full measure of his affection? Underneath the careful script was the equally careful negotiation of emotion—saying too little was better than saying too much. The distance between them went beyond geography, that much was clear, but just as strong was the pull of duty that led him to write his mother and she to read the letter and save it in between the pages of the family Bible. I felt a kinship to Skene, his reticence, and his mystery. Just like Skene's mother, my mother loomed over me and all I was and would not be.

It was then that I asked for a copy of *One Thousand and One Nights,* a request my father gladly fulfilled. At first I thought he was unaware of the racier parts of the book—those parts where salacious women trick their men, losing their morals but gaining the world, but I eventually realized he knew what he was giving me: a trove of tricksterism, a manual for survival. Then I learned of desire, the key to staying alive, the way into the labyrinth, the way out, all the while guzzling life's liquor until it ran dry. Scheherazade, Scheherazade, give me your body, give me your stories or your life. Maybe.

I discovered, too, that desire was the lure of life. To want was to prolong living and to prolong living was to trust the future. The enormity of what a child learns, I think now, is extraordinary. Just as extraordinary is the time spent in coming to terms with all that knowledge. I'm nearly blind. What I imagine I create.

You can't miss what you've never had—all that clutter of images. That others saw much more than I was not my concern. I saw what I saw. Nor did I miss playing baseball or soccer or tennis or badminton, because I'd never learned those games. I found children my age trite and torpid and, more often than not, brutish. They were tiny versions of adults, sans subterfuge. The only game that held my attention was chess, which had been taught to me by Cornelia, a grand lady whose life was truncated by exile. Languages stuck to her like barnacles. She knew half a dozen. Tragedy was her cloak, made of a substance like lead. She led lives like a cat, in Hungary through the German and Soviet occupations, in Austria and Paris, in Madrid, Buenos Aires, Mexico, Havana, and had come to Cubop City aware that this was her last. This city, she'd say in the melancholy tone of the uprooted, has done me in.

It had not done me anything except make me imagine what lay beyond the door, outside our building. While I waited for her to move a piece, I told her stories. Once upon a time, Tuesday refused to go away for three days. Then it was Monday for five minutes, and Sunday appeared in a great expanse of expectation, followed by Wednesday, a block of meat, and

Friday, giddy as a songbird for his mate. It wasn't Saturday for a year and when it came I slept through it. Mama got sick, and soon after, Papa got sick, too, Thursday forever.

Once upon a time there lived a missionary named Skene whose hobby was big-game hunting.

Cornelia looked up from the chessboard. I hadn't shown her the letter.

Missionaries are not big-game hunters, she said.

Why not? I asked.

They're too busy converting the natives.

Okay then, he wasn't a missionary. He was an accountant.

Big-game hunting is an expensive hobby, she said. Only very rich people or famous writers, who live off the rich, can afford it.

Once upon a time there lived a famous writer named Skene Gordon whose hobby was big-game hunting.

Famous? I've never heard of this Skene.

He was famous, I insisted. He'd written many books that were made into movies.

And so it went until she made her move. Then she recited Petőfi in Hungarian and Heine in German. I couldn't understand either language, but her declamations distracted me from the game and I made serious errors, which she exploited with the ruthlessness of a killer.

I couldn't tell her that the real Skene, the one who'd written the letter to his mother, appeared to be a weakling. Big-game hunters are ruthless, with hearts of stone and veins of lead. I remembered a photo from *Hunting in Africa* that showed a hunter aiming his rifle at an elephant as it charged directly at him. If you can shoot an elephant, you can shoot a man, but what pleasure can be derived from that? I kept that to myself while Cornelia thought. What I did say is that Skene shot two elephants as they were mating.

A crack shot, this Skene, she said, still looking at the board. And two beasts at once! Hard to believe.

She moved and quoted Heine's comment that if you can burn a book, you can burn a man. I countered immediately and continued with Skene's story, ignoring her comment. I was much more interested in my narrative than in the game.

Seeing the elephants in death joined as they were in life, Skene so regretted his act that as atonement he joined the National Elephant Preservation Society. Through his activities in the society he met Miss Priscilla Winkley, board member and former president, who became his wife.

No courtship, no romance? Cornelia said, moving one of her knights and threatening my queen.

I got the queen out of harm's way and said there was, but it was irrelevant to the story. Cornelia gave me a stern look and said, How could romance be irrelevant?

On one of their trips to Africa they had a child and Skene became ill. Nevertheless, they lived happily, conjoined by his guilt and their interests, until, finally, he succumbed to his illness and died in his sleep. At the moment of his death, he dreamed he was shot by a hunter of humans while he copulated with an elephant cow who bore an uncanny resemblance to his wife.

How could a man have sex with such a large beast? Cornelia asked. Her voice had cracks in places but was wrapped in elegance. For some reason the thought occurred to me that she was a very lonely woman despite her many lovers.

It was a dream, I said. Dreams don't have logic.

Yes, they do. They may not be linear but they have logic.

A pygmy elephant, then. I was becoming annoyed by her criticisms. In truth, I had never seen a live elephant—only pictures in the encyclopedia and that stunning photograph in *Hunting in Africa*—at close range, so I had no sense of the true size of the animal. I continued. Wracked by grief, Miss Priscilla Gordon, née Winkley, moved to Calcutta and became a Hindu mystic and devotee of Ganesh.

Cornelia pursued my queen. She was relentless.

Is that your story? she asked.

Yes, I said, leaning over the board to see what she'd done.

There is no climax, no great revelation. A story is like love. It rises to a peak of intensity, then comes back down to a state of rest. You must give me more.

I had no idea what Cornelia meant, but in time I learned she was right. Once upon a time you didn't exist.

Mate in three moves.

Once upon a time someone tried to kill you.

A KNIFE ENTERING
THE BELLY

He hasn't known anything like it. There is, first of all, the quick movement of the arm toward his midsection and the flash of metal that protrudes from the balled-up fist. It is the knife blade, of course, and almost simultaneously he knows he is powerless to stop it. He hears an almost inaudible tear as the blade rips through the cotton shirt he's wearing, and then he feels it slice up into the belly through the three layers of skin and into the thoracic cavity. His instinctive reaction is to bend forward and stand on the tip of his toes to keep the blade from going farther. But it is too late for the maneuver. The knife is all the way to the handle, where it stays a moment, then withdraws through the peritoneum, the subcutaneous fat, the dermis, and the epidermis, leaving behind a space that is quickly filled with a burning sensation, like a hot fluid, like blood. There is no pain yet, just a sense of being violated and his head bursting with anger and in his mouth the salt of indignation. He raises his eyes to look at the man's face, but he has already turned away and is fleeing down the street. What? he thinks. What?

He starts walking in the direction of home, and after a few steps his legs grow heavy and unbalanced, his breathing short and insufficient. He doesn't fall so much as float himself down to the sidewalk and sits leaning against a newspaper box. There is a fire in his belly and every breath he takes feeds the flames. He unbuttons his shirt, which is damp and heavy with blood. Each button is an ordeal; each movement of his fingers as they push the buttons through the holes contains all of the pain he has felt in his life to that moment. The wound's small size surprises him, and even in the semidarkness of the city street he can see the blood puddling around the edges and a loop of blue intestine that is protruding through the opening. A wave of embarrassment comes over him and he pushes the intestine back into the stomach. It is not punctured and he is grateful for that. At the same time he thinks that if someone doesn't help him soon he will die, here on the dirty street, the only illumination the copper light at the corner, the only solace the fact that he is dying in the city he loves.

A figure walks by taking fast, loose steps. He mumbles something in the direction of the figure, but there is no response. After some time a couple stops and they bend over him. He can barely raise his eyelids over the balls of his eyes, and his lips and tongue are stuck together with a gummy substance that fills his mouth. The man looks into his face, which must be as pale as the moon right now, and says to the woman, Guy's on some heavy-duty shit. He takes her by the arm and they move quickly away.

He prepares himself to die by looking at the darkened liquor-store window in front of which he has fallen. In one corner of the display is a magnum bottle of Veuve Clicquot, the champagne he once poured over Amanda while she lay in the bathtub. Amanda, the rat, whom he loved beyond expectation, who left him for a young thin boy with sad eyes and unwashed hair, whose absence surrounded him with the scent of solitude. What he wouldn't give to drink that champagne, to have that woman pink and naked before him!

CITY SONG

A city is like a novel. It spreads outward from a starting point, which is where you happen to find yourself when the lights go on: a street late at night, a coffee shop where the night owls are fueling their insomnia, a park where you talk to a mockingbird and the mockingbird talks back, a bar where a man gets shot. Then the city, your city, moves in the direction that is most accessible, away from one moment to the next.

A valleyed city will spread through the valley floor until it runs out of room. It will creep up the hillsides, along natural or artificial terraces, creating tree-lined enclaves for the rich or favelas for the poor. A riparian city will grow along one bank of the river or away from it, depending on the lay. Occasionally it will jump across the water to the other shore, but only if there's a settlement already there and at least one bridge between them that allows for easy travel back and forth. If there is no bridge, one will eventually be built. Ferry travel is slow and boats are subject to the whims of water.

A port city will hug the port, then naturally flow away from it, either along the water's edge or in layers toward the interior, where the food-growing regions lie. In one city the center has moved as the city has grown, leaving behind a series of depressed neighborhoods that once were thriving, barren buildings, meager services, people chewing cud waiting for the machine to start again, and all but empty streets like a backwater. In another city the center stays put. A place like that is fickle and it is only a matter of time before decadence consumes it and all growth stops. That's when the populace begin to move away, in small groups, over time, either to another city where commerce still holds and money still flows, or into the country where they'll be able to relearn the techniques for planting that their families abandoned generations ago, grow their food, and avoid the defeat of a place that crumbles around them even as they try to keep it together, fixing this, patching that, shoring up a balcony, unclogging a sewer pipe.

Some cities live and some cities die; some grow over the ruins of themselves, bearing no relationship to the original other than a dim historical connection and a convenient geographical locus. Ancient and modern Athens. Ancient and modern Rome. Tenochtitlán and Mexico City. Constantinople and Istanbul. Some will disappear altogether, destroyed by war—Troy, Carthage—or by nature—Chichén Itzá, Palenque.

All, however, are driven inexorably by chaos toward decay. On this decay and through it, people live and thrive and die.

Cubop City is all of the above. It is the Dutch and their goats, the English and their teas, Spaniards with their rotten stews, Jews and their lox, Russians and their vodka, Blacks and their kingdom in disguise, poets and plumbers living together, dancers and dentists, actors and accountants and acupuncturists. It is an island between two rivers, a garland around a bay, a glop of concrete on the sand. Cubop City is walking words and static silence and drums and saints and demons with penises like flaming hoses stalking the pretty girls by the school door. It is some skinny lady doing drugs in a bathroom downtown. It is the long nose of the marketplace and the short nose of the church. Cubop City rises out of the stone, rises out of the sea. It grows underground upside down and shoots a million needles into the rapturous sky. Cubop City is that sassy girl slithering onto you like a snake, the man who holds the devil in his hand. Watch his victim dropping to the ground. Watch the pool of blood. Cubop City is blood, a man in a blue bathrobe, a woman who talks to the dead, she knows too much, she loves too much, she dallies through trains and buses and garbage trucks. The killer killed, the wife be done, a man adrift in the sea, a man adrift in himself. The horn plays through the day, the drums at night. The island sinks into memory, memory into sand. Money like water, money like lead, wandering shadows, wandering blind. When baseballs fly out of the sky, when you find your mother crying, your mother gone, a field where your lover turns away, a building on fire, crumbling to dust. A palace of crystal, a Sepharad for the dead, a street that leads to a street that ends in the palace of lye. You go blind. Sun and moon. Mama, Mama. Cubop City. You go blind. Into the underworld, out of the light.

STORYTELLER

The years passed as imperceptibly as dream water. Cornelia stopped coming to the house. It was Mama's doing. She could have her affair with the perfume magnate but she wasn't about to let Papa have his, not in her house. Some things are not to be desecrated as crassly as that. There was no confrontation. One day Cornelia was there; one day she was not. Gone were the chess games. Gone were the quiet moments when we sat across from each other reading silently, gone her passion, barely contained within the trappings of her servitude. She was not beautiful, though I could easily imagine her slim and graceful when young. She was with us seven years. When my manhood began to blossom, currents of desire shot through my body and I fantasized about making love to Cornelia in a room overlooking one of the great European capitals where she'd lived.

She was the loneliest person I have ever known. If you were older, she said to me once, I would fall in love with you. I was shocked. Destitution drove her to passion. That's the way of Europeans. Nevertheless, I was entering the outer boroughs of adulthood and liked hearing that from Cornelia.

I wanted to respond that I didn't need to be older. I let my hand slip over the knuckles and tendons of her hand and let it rest there, until she pulled away and went off to do whatever chore needed doing. She stopped coming to the house soon after and was replaced by a nondescript woman who did her work with a minimum of efficiency and had no poetry to recite, no history to relate. I tried telling her my stories but she grew fidgety and anxious, wanting to get back to her work before the Mr. and Mrs. got home. I told the stories to myself hoping someday I would find someone like Cornelia. Sometimes I made believe I was a nobody living in the greatest city in the world; sometimes I made believe I was an aging professor alone in the city, a boy whose father played baseball with him, a lover of feet, a middle-aged man in love with a twenty-year-old woman, a trumpet player, a struggling writer; mostly I made believe I was myself. The world was made of stories.

Eventually my mother discovered that the new housekeeper had been stealing from us and let her go. They decided a man in his twenties can care for himself, even if he can't see beyond his nose, and they were right. I knew every inch of our apartment. Cornelia had taught me to cook and I was quite at home in the kitchen, able to prepare anything from a chocolate soufflé to a simple omelet, as long as I had the ingredients at hand. If a blind man can play the piano, he can be a good cook. Papa again called me a genius, a culinary phenomenon. He was easy with his words. Mama kept her comments in check, though I heard her once moan with pleasure when she tried my *risotto alla piemontese.*

Life went on in its quiet way, Papa with his students, Mama with her perfume magnate. They didn't entertain much, but when Papa's colleagues from school or Mama's coworkers came for dinner, I cooked *paprikás,* goulash, Dobos cakes, and other dishes Cornelia taught me. The guests marveled that I knew Hungarian cuisine, and I told them I had learned the recipes from an old Hungarian witch. It pleased my mother enormously to hear that. My father clenched his jaw. After my parents got sick, the visits stopped altogether and their friends sent flowers instead. The perfume magnate sent cologne, and the representative of the teacher's union sent a fruitcake on Christmas. Then the cakes stopped coming and all we received were Christmas cards, fewer and fewer every year as we failed to reciprocate and people crossed us off their lists. Eventually, it was just the three of us, marooned in the city of exile.

We lived in an old neighborhood in a prewar building where pieces of plaster fell off the apartment walls, exposing the lath and horsehair filler. Papa was forever calling the superintendent, who ignored the requests to fix the walls as a matter of course, though he once suggested we cover the holes with plastic sheeting, a suggestion Papa tried to implement, nailing the plastic onto the wall and causing more of the plaster to come off. When Mama came home, redolent of perfume and love, she became irate and went downstairs herself and confronted the super, who was, by that point in the day, as high on drugs and alcohol as a functional human being can get. The man went from mumbling incoherencies to complete sobriety after Mama was done with him. He came upstairs with a bucket of plaster and some chicken wire and fixed the holes but not before warning us that the whole building was crumbling.

Building's full of holes, he said. Housing department talking about condemning the property. I fix one hole today and tomorrow another one appears in the hallway. Like cancer.

It was a presage, but like all presages, it didn't feel like one. Just an offhand comment from a crazy, broken-down druggie. As the holes were fixed in the master bedroom, the hallway, and behind the settee in the dining room, the plaster crumbled in other parts of the house—the bathroom, the foyer, the inside of the closet. The superintendent took more drugs when he saw the futility of his work and began to hide from my parents, not answering his door for days at a time. The walls fell away. At dinner we discussed the possibility of moving, but Mama was a headstrong woman who held on to money as if it were a lifeline. In her mind it was the landlord's responsibility to fix the plaster somehow, get another super if need be. She'd start a petition among residents. She'd write a letter to the housing authority. She'd threaten to sue the management company. We were staying put no matter what. Papa got up from the table saying he did not feel well and went to bed.

That was the beginning. Every night after dinner he felt ill and retired early. Every morning he moaned and farted in the bathroom. This went on for two weeks until we found him retching and rolling on the bathroom floor and my mother told him he better get himself to the doctor. He said he couldn't do it by himself; he was in too much pain. So we went together to the emergency room where they gave him morphine and settled him down and did all the tests they had to do. The results came back positive for stomach cancer, incurable since it had metastasized to his intestines. Little to be done but cut away, stuff him full of chemo, and extend his life beyond the six months the oncologist predicted.

Al carajo, Papa said, and after sending the doctors to the deepest pit of hell, he took to bed to wait for his spirit to leave him. Mama, who had been the picture of health in the family to this point, robust in the morning, resplendent in the evening after her sessions with the magnate, took ill, too. It started with a small persistent cough that grew in intensity and kept us awake through the night. The blood came eventually, first in sputa, then in long slivers mixed with her saliva. Back to the doctors again, different ones this time, who pointed to X-rays of her lungs riddled with small white spots—too many tumors to cut out. Mama's verdict was three months. As soon as she heard, she quit her job and went to bed next to Papa, and they both waited for death.

Things happen in threes, people say. We lived in the same space, ate the same food, drank the same water, breathed the same air. I began to feel pain in odd parts of my body. One day it would be the arch of my foot, the next my left arm or my back or deep inside my brain. The pains subsided in a few days and I was left wondering when my time would come, tomorrow, next month, twenty years? It was not something I could tolerate for very long—sitting around waiting, feeding the two death birds, washing and tending to them. The apartment kept falling down around us. Every day there was another hole in the wall, more dust, more plaster on the floor. Once, as I felt my way down the hall toward my parents' bedroom, I touched one of the holes. The different textures brought me to such feelings that I shook uncontrollably and had to use all of my willpower to keep from collapsing. When I recovered I realized I'd come in my pants, without even touching myself, the way I often did while sleeping. I heard my parents calling, but I turned into the bathroom instead, where I washed myself, splashed water on my face, and waited until I could breathe normally again. Then I went into the room and told them the knifing story. I didn't know what else to do.

When I was finished, I noticed Mama's breathing was calmer and Papa's gases had subsided. They asked me what the story meant and I told them I didn't know. It's just a story, I said. Just a story? Papa said. I didn't know how to respond. He embarrassed me. I hadn't yet learned to keep the lion of criticism at bay.

Yes, a little moment, I said.

Not so little, Mama said faintly in a voice that was soft, just this side of tender, not at all like her voice when she came home from the perfume magnate. The man is dying, like we are, except he's on the street.

I think he'll survive, I said.

As if you had any say in the matter, Papa said.

I believe I do. I put him there on that stretch of sidewalk, just as that criminal was walking by intent on doing meanness.

Who was that criminal?

I have no idea. Came out of nowhere.

It was true. I had made up the man and the situation as I sat before my parents in a narrative trance, making believe I was telling Cornelia the story while I waited for her to move a chess piece.

Well, I need to know who he was, Mama piped in. I could hear tiny wheezes punctuating her words.

Give me some time. I'll tell you another story tomorrow.

Then they both grew quiet. Mama turned to look out the window at the mottled sky. Papa lay with his eyes closed, snoozing. And then I understood what would happen if I told them a story, or part of a story, every day. It wasn't a cure for their maladies but a way of existing, going from story to story as Cornelia went from city to city as her condition dictated and her needs allowed. In Paris she was a femme fatale. In Havana she was an exotic European. In Cubop City she was a servant, a lover of husbands and poetry. One more day taken from death was one more day of memory, of staying alive.

I made believe I could see, I made believe I was a character in the stories. I made believe I had a life inside the fiction, that I could love and be afraid and tell stories and be wounded and married and divorced and live alongside the characters I created. And that it was all true.

CORNELIA'S STORY

Loss is my secret name. In the war I lost the land that had been in my family since the days of the empire. I lost my husband and children. I lost my dignity the way women do at the hands of victorious soldiers. I resisted at first, but they beat me until my mouth bled and there was a constant ringing in my ear. The ringing drowned out the moans of the soldiers. After the third one I felt nothing. When the fifth came along, I helped him unbuckle his pants. He was very young and nervous and had never been with a woman. A captain appeared and put a stop to the affair, threatening to shoot the next man who came close to me.

Out of habit more than hygiene, I washed myself and found a dress in the clothes chest the Germans had not stolen, a white dress with violet trim that smelled of mothballs. My husband gave it to me for our tenth anniversary. His secret name was give, my children his greatest gift. I thought maybe the future would bring a life outside the nightmare. Perhaps the nightmare was all anyone had a right to expect and life in it was better than no life at all.

The next day I cleaned the house and the garden, what was left of it, and hired a girl from the village to help me. I promised her a salary as soon as money came my way. The soldiers had not touched the stables, and there were several saddles and reins I could sell and a good anvil and forging tools the village blacksmith would pay for, even if it was in next-to-worthless pengös. The village girl loved getting those pieces of colored paper. I counted them out on her palm and she folded them and put them inside her dress, an awful green dress.

That afternoon the German officer returned and apologized for all his men did to me. He said war turns men into beasts, as if that excused them. He asked if there was anything I needed. I told him I had no food, and the next day the captain's adjutant appeared with potatoes, onions, and flour, followed by tea, tobacco, and brandy the day after. Toward the end of the week the captain himself came and he brought a large kolbász. I wanted to take that kolbász from his hand and bite into it right away, but I controlled myself and asked him in. Hunger drove me, nothing else. Right then the captain was my savior. I served him some tea with a touch of brandy, along with the kolbász and slices of peasant bread the village girl had baked. He spoke of the war. I listened, not caring much what he said, and ate the sausage and the bread, trying to be decorous. He was from Stuttgart, an engineer by training. He worked for

27

Mercedes-Benz. When he left at dusk he took my hand, bowing toward it as if to kiss it. I pulled it away. With my stomach full I had the luxury of hating him. Yet, at the same time, I recognized in him a certain grace, which predated the war to a time when such behavior was the norm. The captain was an educated man. I missed educated people and found myself hoping he would return.

That he did, every afternoon. My loneliness was greater than my rage. We spoke about literature and music and my years studying in Germany. He spoke of his wife and children and I told him how my husband and sons were killed when a German plane bombed the train they were on. He was very sorry and tried to console me. He mused about the sadness of war, the distances it made, the chasms it created. He seemed wistful. I thought he must be a terrible soldier. Once soldiers kill, they keep killing. I've seen it. This captain wasn't like that. He was tormented. I couldn't hate him.

I changed the conversation and recited a poem by Heine. He mocked my Hungarian accent and we laughed—rare thing then, to laugh. He asked if he could kiss me and I said yes and responded more ardently than I would have imagined a week before. He asked if we could make love. His words were not those of an officer in the German army but of a man tired of slaughter and longing. I was destitute and desperate for kindness. I whispered yes—*igen*—and then in German—*ja*. I took him by the hand—he had long, elegant fingers—and led him to the bedroom, where we made love as people in a war make love, knowing only the present and promising each other nothing.

One day the captain stopped coming and the Germans withdrew, driven away by the Russians. They came in a large wave of conquering they called liberation. They parceled out my land among the peasants. They gave them flags to wave and hymns to sing and told them it was their turn now—the dictatorship of the proletariat—and the peasants were happy even though they didn't know what that meant. Worse than the Germans they were, dirty Cossacks. They shat everywhere, in my garden, whatever was left of it, on the fields the Germans had destroyed, in back of the house by the well, even on the porch. I went to see the Russian officers and pleaded with them to build latrines. The accumulation of the feces of five thousand men is something to be reckoned with. Despite the latrines, my land, or what had been my land, and the village, or what had been the village, began to resemble hell. This is the dictatorship of defecation, I told the Russian officers, in Hungarian, of course, so they wouldn't understand.

Someone in the village informed the Russians of the captain's visits and charged me with collaboration. The Russians sat complacently in my chairs and heard me defend myself. I asked them to speak to a family of Jews that had survived in the village. I'd given them food and found them a barn where they could hide. They vouched for me. The Jews were sent east and were never heard from. I was left alone for the time being. I was allowed a room in the back of the house, which I left only to retrieve the remnants of vegetables that grew in the garden and the scraps of food the village girl passed on to me when the Russians were asleep or drunk on their vodka.

The Russians raped me, too, but by then I was smart enough to negotiate. When one of them, a lanky fellow with an empty look in his eye, wanted me to fellate him, I asked for a bottle of vodka, which I could trade for food. He agreed but when he was done he gave me only half a liter. I took a swig, swirled it in my mouth, and spit it out. At that moment I decided I would leave my house and my country and never return, no matter what I found elsewhere. The next day, at first light, I packed a valise with some clothes and jewelry I had hidden away under the floorboards, and walked out to the main road. No one stopped me.

In those days following the war, entire populations were moving. The city dwellers who'd been displaced to the countryside were wandering back to the cities, only to find ruins. The country folk returning to their farms found them overgrown and fallow, their houses pilfered for wood, their orchards cut down or trampled. I saw empty towns, empty faces, a man without shoes crawling on hands and knees, women lying on the side of the road, too tired to take another step, an awful look in their eyes, and a pack of hungry dogs circling around them. I saw columns of Russian soldiers going in one direction and columns of American soldiers going the opposite way. The Americans waved and smiled and offered chewing gum. So this is victory, I thought.

I was in Vienna for two months, almost starving amid the defeat of a beautiful city, and from there I went to Paris. From Paris I traveled to Lisbon and from Lisbon by boat to Havana.

I survived by taking on lovers, of which I had plenty—brutes, dandies, intellectuals, idiots, savants, dullards, men of substance, wispy men, one assassin that I knew of, one potential saint, several homosexuals, and three women of different ages. Some might say I was a kept woman, but I never stayed anywhere long enough to earn that title. In Havana I found a mason. He had rough hands and an eager heart. I was as unstable as a sand dune blown by the wind, and soon I abandoned the mason for a politician. Like all his breed the politician was a chameleon, changing color to suit his circumstance, wanting money more than votes and power more than money. Most of all he longed for approval. He was in love with me as he was in love with several other women, including his wife, and never doubted the legitimacy of his love or the constancy of his multiple affections. My affair with him might have gone on forever, even into old age, but one day he found himself pursued by enemies intent on his elimination. He escaped into exile in the United States with his wife and three daughters and a suitcase full of cash.

One of the last things the politician did before leaving was get me a job teaching philosophy at the university. It was there I met Vicente Iriarte, the anatomy professor, early in the first term. He was a pale man with thinning black hair that he combed straight back and held down with pomade. Out of his nostrils grew tufts of nose hairs and on his face was a permanent five-o'clock shadow that gave him the appearance of a sinister cobbler. But Vicente was a jovial and cultured man who could recite Schiller in German and sing Italian arias in our bedroom. His large belly bounced when he laughed, which he did loudly and often. His laughter was the perfect antidote to the dark moods I had dragged from Europe like a chain of misery around my neck.

After work he would sit in the front porch to catch the afternoon breeze and I would bring him a beer, then go back in to cook for him those casseroles and stews Cubans liked to eat in those days when food was plentiful, as well as Hungarian peasant dishes my mother's gypsy cooks had taught me—he liked those, too. I learned to please him sexually, rubbing his fantastical belly, then moving my hand down to find his little nub hidden in a nest of pubic hair. Once he got hard I mounted him and rode him until he giggled, laughed, squealed, and came in quick spasmodic jerks of his pelvis. He fell asleep quickly and I took care of myself. It was best that way. I'd reached the age when I knew my body better than any man. All I wanted now was the erasure of the past that I had been seeking all the years after the war, through all the cities I'd passed, people I'd loved or who had loved me. In Havana the darkness dissipated, the glue dissolved. I began inching my way toward hope. No one suffers forever, I told myself, not even Job. I was wrong.

Off in the mountains there was a rebel army fighting the government, and in the city student groups were leading demonstrations, attacking police barracks and stations, planting bombs in shopping areas. As a professor I was asked to provide funds, hide guns, and give the student leaders passing grades. I refused. Not that I was against their ideals, no. Ideals are good in young minds. I was simply tired of war. My family was dead. My land was gone, my country, or what had been my country, under the heel of the Soviets. The police responded as police everywhere respond—by rounding up suspects, torturing and killing them at random, and dropping their bodies on street corners and parks. I knew how all this would end. I told Vicente but he reassured me that these upheavals were part of life in Cuba. Our society needs cleansing every few years, he said. Things will settle down, the students will go back to their studies, and the unionists will return to work.

I distracted myself with Vicente and my German students, whom I taught privately at home. I took up sewing and wrote poetry. I could feel the breath of the past on my neck.

Vicente was mistaken. The revolutionaries triumphed and the country went on a binge of celebration. The university closed its doors and on every street corner were groups of armed men, all young, puffed up with victory. I wanted to leave the country. Vicente was dismissive in his jovial way. You can't run away every time there's trouble. It was easy for him to say that. Cuba was his country, not mine. I had no interest in any struggle except self-preservation. I insisted.

Where would we go? he asked. We were sitting on the front porch. Vicente was wearing a sleeveless T-shirt tucked tightly into his gray pants. The flab of his belly flopped over his belt. He had just taken a shower and his black hair glistened in the late afternoon sunlight. There is no better place than this, he said, moving his arm in front of him in an arcing motion.

Al norte, I said. The United States was not a place I had thought of living in. It had just occurred to me because so many Cubans were going there at the time.

What will we do, work in a factory? he said. For once I saw him angry. Sweat was beading on his forehead and the tip of his nose had turned red. He paused to compose himself. No, we stay here.

I wanted to tell him the victors can do anything they want. I wanted to tell him about all I'd gone through at their hands, but I refrained. Vicente waved me away, laughing. How could he understand? All that mirth made him light-headed. I held my tongue and went inside to make dinner.

That night after Vicente fell asleep I made the decision to leave as soon as I could. It was difficult to abandon him, but it would be more difficult to stay behind and wait for the tide of loss to swallow me. The following week, when he'd gone downtown to meet a friend, I packed my old leather valise and left a farewell note. There are things that have no solutions, I wrote, and solutions that are worse than the problems they are meant to resolve. I thanked him for his attentions. I did not write the word *love*.

I arrived in Cubop City in February, and my tropical clothes, mostly cotton and linen dresses, were inadequate for the weather. I spent fifty dollars on a coat and gloves and rented a room in a residential hotel on the West Side. I knew how to make my money last. Finding a job was easy. I played stupid. I did not list my doctorate in the application, and in two days I was working for a temp agency. It was a job as jobs go and it paid my bills. When someone called the agency asking for a European nanny to care for a blind boy, I volunteered for it immediately. I was, after all, the only European there. I lied that I had plenty of experience in Hungary and Cuba, where I'd served as private tutor for the children of a prominent family.

I told my boss I spoke five languages—that was no lie. He was unbelieving; nevertheless he allowed me to go to the interview.

The couple who interviewed me were Cubans of the old order who expected me to do housecleaning and food preparation and laundry and silver polishing, chores hardly befitting a private tutor. I was about to excuse myself and walk away when the boy appeared in the living room. He walked directly to me, stiff backed and mechanical, and put out his hand for me to shake. His blurred eyes and smeared eyelids startled me, but the delicacy of his voice awakened in me the maternal instinct I had long suppressed. It entered my mind that he would make a good dog. I took the job.

The mother was a stern woman who spoke in commandments. You will do this, you will not do that. Whatever love existed in her had long ago been burned out. The father turned out to be needier than the son. He was a good, sweet man who tolerated his wife and her infidelity because he didn't know what else to do. I took him out of loneliness and charity, but he turned out to be a good lover, willing to please me before pleasing himself. He was a teacher and got home before the wife. That allowed us some time together and we made love quietly so as not to disturb the boy in his room. I think he heard us anyway. It was a different matter the few times the father came to my apartment. There we gave vent to our passion. Eventually the wife became suspicious, feigned outrage, and fired me. That same night I had a dream of a black bridge stretching back to Europe. I was sorry to leave the blind boy who was smart and gentle. He moved in and out of happiness and was desperate to know the world. I was sorry to leave the father. I felt pity for him mostly. The mother was a witch who had a love affair with her boss. Her commandments did not apply to her.

I found myself out of a job and had prospects for none. For weeks I lost track of myself. I would wake in my apartment and not know what I'd done or where I'd been. Sometimes I smelled of liquor and cigarettes; other times of sex. On the bed lingered the scent of strangers. I found piles of unopened bills on the table by the door and food spoiling in the refrigerator. My clothes were scattered on the floor and the bed was a jumble of sheets and pillows. Beyond myself with fear at what I'd done in my amnesia, I called my former lover, the Cuban teacher with the blind son, who gave me the name of a psychiatrist and hung up.

The suggestion that I needed a psychiatrist struck me as absurd. It was God who needed one, not I. God, the miserly master with the wide buttocks and the huge testicles, sat on his sofa and fanned himself as the world burned. All this time I'd expected him to come down in his mercy machine and make my life tolerable. Life is neither tolerable nor intolerable. It just is; otherwise, I wouldn't have come to be in that room at that time in this city. I opened the blinds and let the morning light flood in. I surveyed my apartment and thought of fleeing as I'd fled other disasters, but I didn't. I showered and put on the last clean dress I owned. Then I cleaned as I'd never cleaned before, even when I was with Vicente and it was my happiness to do so. That simple act did more to bring me back to my senses than all the roaming I'd done and all the lovers I'd had over the years.

All the money I had was in my purse, enough for breakfast and a newspaper. As I ate, I leafed through the classified ads and found my current job, which I've had for fifteen years arranging tours for people who like to visit the world I left behind. They find it quaint, restored to a postcard version of what it once was. They don't know about the ruins on which that world is built. They don't know about the hunger or the splinters of souls that litter the ground on which they walk, or about the walking dead, like me, for whom Cubop City is a last resort. We are born again here. We take our first steps. We learn the new language, the rhythms of the days and nights, the hymns of false virtue that keep us in our place, moving nowhere but deeper into ourselves, where a minotaur waits.

A WHITE BIRD
CROSSING THE SKY

Angel didn't die. Eventually a Good Samaritan passed by, saw his bloody shirt, his bloody belly, his body splayed on the sidewalk against the newspaper box, and called the police. The pedestrian crouched over him, his hand resting softly on Angel's shoulder until the officers came. Angel didn't learn the name of the man who saved his life. Now that Angel is healthy, the pedestrian comes to him in dreams; he is sometimes long and lanky, sometimes short and round, holding a cell phone to his ear. Behind him a crowd is pointing and gesticulating in Angel's direction. The crowd has no faces, only hands and fingers. They don't bother lowering their voices, and they all speak together, making it impossible for him to make out individual words or the sense of what they're saying. Rutabaga, watermelon. Even if he could, it wouldn't much matter.

Soon the emergency medical technicians gather around him to work on his wound and the crowd disperses into the night.

At this point the dream takes one of three routes: the route of the desert, the route of water, or the route of dissipation. The first is self-evident. He is in the Atacama, the Sahara, the Mojave. The heat sears his skin and his thirst makes his tongue swell with pustules. Off in the distance there are blue mountains he never reaches no matter how much he walks. Shadows don't exist there, not even his own, and when he turns to look back from where he's come, he realizes he hasn't moved an inch since yesterday. He tells himself that he must complain to the proper authorities, but they will not pay attention to him, limited as they are by the rules of their office. Forms in triplicate. Sleepy clerks. Appeals to the assistant deputy superintendent.

In the second he finds himself snorkeling in water so clear it is like dense air. The fish are plentiful. They get in the way; they nip at his skin. He sees a manta ray the size of a car flap by under him; he sees moray eels and green and yellow sea snakes and a twenty-foot shark swallowing a brown grouper. Without realizing it he has swum several hundred yards away from the shore, past the continental shelf. When he looks down, what faces him is bottomless ocean, deep blue, all-encompassing, and he falls into the eye that is looking at him.

The third dream is the one Angel longs for most and the one he is most reticent to enter. When it happens, he is drinking champagne with Amanda in a room where everyone is naked except them. After a few minutes a blonde-haired woman approaches the two of them and asks them in a gentle but insistent tone to take off their clothes. She is helping Angel unzip his pants when suddenly a rabbit bloops out the fly. She laughs and throws the rabbit into the air. Amanda is looking at this with a smile or a grimace on her face—he can't tell. She asks him if he knows the woman, and he says there is something familiar about her but that no, really, he has never seen her before. In some versions of the dream Amanda catches the rabbit and is petting it. In another variation the woman with blonde hair is Angel's wife and Amanda is in love with her. She pulls her away from him and takes her to the sofa, where they have sex. Usually a dead fish makes its way into the dream, wrapped in newspaper or hanging from a hook, and off in the distance there is a beautiful beach on which soft, creamy waves are breaking. What wakes him: a white bird crossing the sky.

THE CITY OF
THE PRESENT

Each day you wake to a landscape that has followed you since childhood. Each morning you miss the songs of mockingbirds you heard many years ago when you lived by the river. What you hear instead are the garbage trucks of America, their grating roar, and the honk of taxis, impatient yellow geese, and the banter of drunken children going home at dawn to anxious parents in the suburbs. You are not of this place and so you can only pine for those early days, finding yourself awake in the same spot, the city of the present and the city of the past repeated again and again as if they were practices of memory trapped in reality.

The city now is ahead of itself. Deeply wounded, it has healed. What is left is a scar, a raw, hard place on the skin, and the airplanes crashing into buildings and the smoke billowing and the ashes settling on the cemetery. One third of the people want to cover up the hole as if it never existed; another group wants to dig inside, keep the wound open, let it suppurate until it infects the abdominal cavity; the last third doesn't know what is best. They go to their jobs in the morning, return home at night, live the everyday life in suspension between the idyllic past and the lurching future, and hope that from the constancy comes the antidote against the claims of time. What none of them knows is that over the actual city there is a primal city that will outlive them. They inhabit both, one as a function of their geographical selves, that is, creatures who either find themselves accidentally among its structures or have actually sought it out for its familiarity; the other in relation to their function as businessmen, construction workers, writers, cooks, crane operators, hot-dog vendors, sausage makers, ballet dancers, window cleaners, priests, simultaneous interpreters, brick layers, bridge painters.

At lunch you overhear a conversation between two friends about seducing a landlady. Friend number one wants nothing more than to have her turn off her radio. She plays an oldie station with the volume loud enough that he has trouble concentrating. Listen, he tells his friend. I could do it. She's still attractive; she must have been beautiful as a young woman.

How old is she? the friend asks.

Oh, sixty maybe.

That's tough. What makes you think she'll turn the radio down instead of up?

She's sublimating. As soon as she has good sex, she'll do anything I say.

What if she gives better sex than she gets? friend number two says. Will you then do anything for her, will you let her turn the volume up even higher?

At this point their soup comes and their conversation drifts here and there—work, new apartment, baseball—with nothing to hold it together.

You move into your own mind. No one would deny you're from Cubop City, even if you were born elsewhere. When you came thirty-eight years ago, you were twelve. There was no anxiety about how to get around, how to act, what to say. You knew these things, you had learned the code in the city of your birth, and you applied it with relative success. There were minor adjustments. In Cubop City you didn't have to wave at buses for them to stop. You had to look carefully before crossing a street; there was less sky to look at, more anger to avoid. There were crowds at rush hour such as you'd never seen. Minor things. You knew the pulse of the city because it was your pulse. You knew to get out of harm's way, yell at a driver running a yellow light. Your heart beat fast; your ambition grew in direct relation to the city itself, its thirst and hunger, its drive to charge at nature and swallow it. The city was hard work, propelling itself beyond the day to the next at the speed of neon. In winter, bundles moved about spewing steam like locomotives. The sun was weak willed and timorous. The city went on with its business.

You finish your lunch and walk outside. It is autumn. Already the saplings on the avenue have lost their leaves. The noise has grown and you feel the need for quiet, the afternoon scurrying away into the factory towns of New Jersey, the body of time stretching as a cat stretches on the floor. We can only remember the past: a slow movie about to end, the smell of ripe guava, the taste of tamarind, a mockingbird swooping to a fence post, marking territory with song. You are walking down the sidewalk, the primal and the actual city intertwined. The organism that took your childhood away is the one that gave you the gift of manhood. You will know no other place like you know this. This city with a scar like a knife wound on its belly, this city like the flames shooting into the sky, rock hewn, crystallizing, into which you disappear.

THE BUTTERFLY

After the knifing, when Angel is so close to death he can taste its breath, a field opens before him and slopes down to the sea. He goes out on that field and sits in the tall grass. The sky is deep blue and the sun is a friendly creature with no inclination to blaze. Hours he spends looking out toward the water, reclining backward with elbows on the ground. Sometimes an orange butterfly alights on his bare knees and its scratchy legs distract him from his reverie. Is the butterfly imagining him, or is he imagining the butterfly? It is very beautiful and seems comfortable there. Even as he thinks comfortable, he wonders if that isn't fallacious. Comfort doesn't enter into the life of an insect any more than it enters into the life of a rock. Butterfly is still one moment, in motion the next. It has no expectation of comfort, no way of identifying it. Then the thought occurs to him, as spontaneously as the butterfly, that all qualities he applies to himself and his fellow humans—there is that beautiful neighbor getting into her car with that sullen expression; there is the rapacious building manager who is trying to get him out of his apartment; there is a broken woman making her way through the world—are in the end manifestations of that same pathetic fallacy. Sometimes he thinks his feelings are chemical impulses not much different from the ones that drive the butterfly, except that he is aware of them, an awareness that often leads to paralysis, though he might call it comfort.

His mind returns to the field, the way it slopes gently toward the water and then, with a sudden dip, reaches the sand. Yellow flowers, the names of which he doesn't know, sway in the breeze. Overhead a hawk is thermalling, and far away on the ocean's surface tiny sailboats are flashing in the sun. Off the corner of his eye he notices a figure dressed in white looking at him. This story was going to be about her and about the small house they share on the hill. It is there where he is trying to recreate the universe in his image, but every day it becomes more arduous, less like him and increasingly like a broken atomized picture where only his chin or his ears or his shadowed brow or sometimes a tooth or half a tongue is identifiable. Behind the hill on which the house sits are two ridges. A trestle bridge crosses from one ridge to the other, and it is rumored that in the old days, young pregnant women threw themselves off it into the path of oncoming trains. Nothing of the sort has happened since they've been here.

The white figure that appeared on the edge of the field is his lover. She has been very good to him, keeping the house in order and making suggestions as he goes about recreating the universe. As he said, it is a difficult process and he simply cannot keep track of everything. One day he puts a gun on the table on one page and on the next he has a vase of flowers. Guns to roses? No. Sloppiness. Or a character is blonde in chapter 3 but dark haired in chapter 5. Once, he created the character of a priest who was the embodiment of goodness itself. A few pages later, the priest was unexpectedly found in bed with his niece. It was as if the universe, infinite in its possibilities, kept intruding on the fiction—no, on his writerly mind—and insisted on fighting the convolutions of actuality with the artifice of linear narrative. His lover has been quite helpful in pointing these things out and quite helpful, too, in the subtle ways in which she eases him when the writing is not going well. Just last week, for example, before she went out for the day, she left lunch on the table and next to it the Hemingway book open to his favorite passage of "Big Two-Hearted River." He ate lunch at ten in the morning and spent the rest of the day reading and rereading that passage.

After the dishes are done, an antediluvian quiet settles over the house. The crickets chirp and a whip-poor-will sings. His lover and he sit on the sofa and discuss the next day's work. Her docility then is in contrast to the catlike spirit that leaps out of her in moments of anger or when she abandons herself to the pleasures of the bed. She's had plenty of experience with other lovers, but it is mostly instinct that drives her, not knowledge. He's flesh in her maw and he submits. She keeps him from falling into the abyss of the birds without caring what is eternal: joy or terror. Love comes in many guises.

47

As she approaches he notices that her face bears an expression he's never seen before, a stony indifference, a stern determination. Her steps are not languorous but forceful, martial even, as if she were following the orders of a higher force. When she reaches him, she looks down, and for a moment he can see the wings of pity fly across her eyes, but they are soon replaced by a rapine shadow that presses him down and keeps him on the ground in the same position from which he has been admiring the sea and the sailboats.

Oh, she's come to tell him that she cannot live with him anymore, that she has found someone else, etc., etc. She will leave today with her clothes and some of the things he has given her. He feels as if he must get up and be at eye level with her, but her gaze, which he himself has made all-powerful, pins him to the ground. She turns, and in her turning is such grace he can barely stand it. His heart is beating fast and his throat wants to crumble, but if he has one advantage over the situation, it is that everything around him is his making—the house, the field, the sea, his posture, his lover walking toward him and walking away.

He lets her go and lies back to look at the sky, which is soon covered by clouds. A strong wind blows off the ocean and the butterfly disappears. The wind pushes the grass stalks uphill and in a few minutes large drops start falling, a few at first, and then the sky breaks open and the rain comes down, heavy, persistent. He runs back to the house and finds that everything is as he left it, the whiskey bottle on the counter, the red roses he bought yesterday, still fresh and fragrant, the cantaloupe half on the kitchen table that he hoped they could have with lunch. Sitting on the reading chair he listens to the rain hit the cottage roof, beating him down until he is a small helpless creature in the universe of his making. He realizes his love, that he himself devised, is a dull sublunary lovers' love.

KILLER OF
CROCODILES

Angel's grandfather, Pedro Romero, was the best policeman in Havana. They say he wasn't afraid of anyone, un macho de verdad, they say, driven to ridding the city of the criminal elements who dominated the streets, even if he had to break the law to do so. Angel met Pedro in a nursing home in Miami, thirty years after Angel's grandmother threw him out of the house for his philandering ways. Pedro took up with a woman with whom he had a daughter, and after she, too, broke with him, he fake-married a simple twenty-year-old girl from the country. They say his cousin, Gustavo, a lawyer and notary public, arranged the whole thing but never submitted the papers to the marriage bureau, so as far as the law was concerned, the marriage never took place. Pedro was merely interested in getting the guajira into bed. He wound up falling in love and stayed with her for fifteen years until he left for the United States. By then he had retired from the police force but his reputation preceded him everywhere he went. He was, after all, the man who had tracked, found, and killed Manolito Rivas, one of the most notorious murderers ever to roam the streets of the capital. Whenever Pedro entered a bar, people bought him drinks, and more than once he was seen walking down the Malecón with a tall, blonde Americana on his arm.

By the time Angel met Pedro he'd been writing for ten years. He'd published two books that sold a total of a thousand copies, give or take a dozen, and after considering his meager success, he was almost ready to give up writing for good. His ambition, his last thread of hope, was to write a story about Pedro that would revive his sputtering writer's soul.

Pedro was a shriveled old man who could hardly speak due to the laryngeal cancer that was killing him but who still whistled at all the nurses who entered his room, even the ugly ones. As a result the nurses gave him special treatment, bringing him chocolate treats to suck on and cans of Orange Crush, the only liquid that slaked his ever-present thirst. When he saw Angel, he raised his hands in an inquiring gesture, and Angel answered that he was Zoila's grandson and therefore his as well. Pedro started shaking so badly that he had to sit down. He waved Angel over to the chair and embraced him, planting a wet, unpleasant kiss on his cheek. Then he told that old joke about an inventor who had developed a fruit that tasted like a woman's vagina. Angel forced out a laugh.

You don't like the joke? he asked. Angel could practically hear his vocal chords straining to vibrate.

I've heard it before, Angel said.

The truth was that laughing was difficult because Angel had inherited his family's resentment over the way Pedro had treated them. What kind of man would abandon his wife and children just like that? His father was forced to leave school and work sweeping the floors of a soap factory at fourteen, and his uncle was so traumatized by the absence of a father that he started drinking at sixteen, and by the time he was twenty-five he was a hopeless dipsomaniac. Angel's grandmother, Zoila, became a recluse, embittered by what Pedro had done yet unable to forget the only man who had brought any kind of happiness to her life. As she drew her last breath she called out: Pedro, *ven a mí*. Come to me.

How is your grandmother? Pedro asked, looking at Angel intently.

She's fine, Angel lied and quickly changed the conversation. Manolito Rivas, the famous murderer. You found him?

Yes, he said and then remained silent for some time. His eyes were frozen and unmoored. His jaw dropped open.

If the old man dies now, Angel thought, I won't get my story, and so he called out to him several times until he awoke.

Did you hear the one about Mr. Pérez and Mr. Brown at a bar in South Miami? Pedro asked.

Angel listened to the joke and this time he laughed heartily. He waited a few minutes before asking Pedro again to tell him about his pursuit of Manolito Rivas.

Pedro smiled, his eyes fixed on the wall by the door, then shook his head slowly as if remembering something fanciful, a story he had once invented to entertain friends but which had now become more real than the rest of his life. He opened a fresh can of Orange Crush and began to speak.

Manolito Rivas was a dandy, always dressed impeccably in the latest styles. His hair was slicked back and shiny, and his fingernails were perfectly manicured. To see him walking down the street you'd think he was a successful actor or musician or a child of privilege. In reality he was a brutal killer, murdering women with impunity and then boasting about his exploits in the barrios of the city. Despite his life of crime, maybe because of it—you never know about these things—Manolito Rivas had become a legend in Havana. Newspapers carried front-page stories about his antics—how he'd set a woman on fire after raping her; how he'd enamored the scion of a wealthy banking family, then drowned her in the bathtub and distributed her money among the poor who lived in La Plaza del Vapor. His last victim was the widow of a government retiree whom he'd suffocated and then shoved her dentures down her throat. What a way to die, devoured by your own mouth!

At this point Pedro had a coughing fit and he had to stop. When Angel asked him if he should get the nurse, Pedro waved his hand dismissively and took several sips of his Orange Crush until he settled down.

All the city newspapers fulminated against police incompetence. Politicians' switchboards lit up with calls from worried citizens. Finally, at the urging of the First Lady, who became convinced no woman was safe as long as Manolito Rivas roamed the streets, the president himself demanded immediate action. That's when the police chief called Pedro, whose honesty and peculiar adherence to the law had won him the respect of his peers. Pedro had been whiling away his time in Vedado, an upper-class neighborhood of Havana, where he arrested petty thieves, gave them a good beating, and sent them home with the warning that next time he would not be so lenient. Vedado was a highly coveted assignment in those days as the residents were fond of tipping the police generously to take special care of their properties. Pedro came home every night with wads of cash stuffed in his pockets, making Zoila the happiest woman on her block. Pedro, however, had not joined the police force to be rich but to be respected. And so, when the police chief offered him the Manolito Rivas case, he jumped at the opportunity.

At this point Pedro pointed at his throat and made a grimace. He got up from his chair, lay down on the bed, and promptly fell asleep. Not wanting to return to the nursing home, Angel waited for a while hoping that he would wake, rested and ready to continue his story, then resigned himself to the fact that he'd have to come the next day.

That night, after too many drinks, Angel asked his father what he remembered about Pedro. His father poured himself a whiskey and said that Pedro seemed intent on ridding Havana of undesirable elements and was always running after some criminal or other, sometimes not coming home for days at a time. When he did, he was usually too tired to talk to his children, instead changing into his pajamas and going straight to bed without so much as a hello or a good-night. He was not a good father, his father said and asked Angel why he was digging all this up now. I'm writing a story about him, Angel said, and his father responded that he'd rather he wrote a story about someone not in the family. Family matters are private. Then he changed the conversation to a real-estate deal he had just closed in Hialeah.

Angel awoke the next morning with a bad headache and a worse disposition and waited until the middle of the afternoon to return to the nursing home. Pedro was not in his room and for a moment Angel worried that he might have died during the night. It was not a worry he entertained very long. Angel found him in the recreation room surrounded by a group of residents. With his Orange Crush can next to him on a table, Pedro stood in front of his aluminum walker telling them jokes. His audience sat in their wheelchairs as if transfixed, but on closer look Angel realized that most of them were barely conscious. Only one of them was smiling, permanently, a string of saliva dripping down onto a plastic bib.

When Pedro saw Angel he smiled and waved him over. His voice was less scratchy that day, and he proudly introduced Angel to the group as his grandson, the famous writer. There was no response from any of them except for a small fellow in the back who started hiccupping and was soon led away by one of the nurses.

You want to tell them a joke? Pedro asked his grandson.

He said he wasn't good at jokes.

It doesn't matter, Pedro said. Their minds are gone. They can't tell the difference between a joke and a sermon.

Now Angel was on the spot. His headache was returning and his mouth was as dry as chalk. Angel told the one about the two drunks who think they are climbing the stairway to heaven but are merely crawling on a railroad track. Not even Pedro cracked a smile.

You weren't kidding, he said. Are you sure you're my grandson?

They went back to his room, where, without any prodding on Angel's part, Pedro continued the story.

Manolito Rivas was as slippery as an eel and blatant as a foghorn. No sooner did you think you had him cornered than a mist of uncertainty would surround you. He was here, he was there, he was everywhere. One day you heard he was in El Cerro entertaining the neighbors by singing boleros with a street band; the next someone had caught sight of him miles away playing dice at a bodega in Jaimanitas. Finally, after many weeks of work, I found Manolito in a rented room in the Colón district as he was dressing to go on his evening rounds. I showed him my badge and pointed my gun right at his heart. Manolito smiled, one leg in his pants, the other out, and said, I am a real criminal and I am not surrendering. You are a real cop. Shoot me.

I did. End of story.

Angel had heard from both his uncle and grandmother when she was alive that Pedro had spent weeks searching for the killer, disguising himself as a bourgeois matron, a streetwalker, even a nun, in hopes of catching Manolito in the act. Pedro had become a regular at several bordellos that the criminal was rumored to frequent, leading Zoila to exclaim that it was more than his duty that her husband was performing. Angel's uncle added that when Pedro ran out of leads, he would ride trolleys from one end of the city to another at all hours, hoping to catch sight of the killer. Once, Pedro disguised himself as a guajiro, a country bumpkin, replete with straw hat, leggings, and machete, and took his two sons, then seven and eight years old, to La Concha, the public beach where he had heard Manolito Rivas would sometimes go for a swim, and there the three of them spent the day frying in the sun.

When Angel asked Pedro why he did all of this, he shook his head and dismissed it with a wave of the hand.

Part of the work, he said. Part of the work. The important thing is that I caught and killed him.

Did you feel any remorse about shooting him? Angel asked.

What kind of question is that?

Well, you killed a human being.

Pedro looked at Angel as if he were mentally deficient. I killed a crocodile, he said.

That night as Angel sat in his father's backyard drinking a Materva and waiting for the heat to abate, he considered what Pedro had said. For him, being a policeman, whether apprehending a burglar or shooting a criminal, was a matter of duty. Simple. Why couldn't Angel think that way? Why couldn't writing be his duty? He avoided the issue by calling Luli, a former lover of his he hadn't seen in five years, and asking her to have a drink with him. She'd been supportive of his work back then and he thought she'd be supportive of it now. He needed something simple. As they shared mojitos in Coral Gables, Angel asked her what she thought of him as a writer.

I think you're a two-timing hijo de puta.

As a writer, damn it!

Do you know what you put me through?

Yes. But if you can put that aside for a moment . . .

Of course she couldn't. She downed her third mojito, picked up her purse, and left the bar. His instinct was to run after her and apologize. Despite her forty-plus years, her body was still shapely and her face glowed with sensuality. He was lonely. He remembered their days of passion and glory when they made the bed levitate and angels and demons dance cheek to cheek around them, but he stayed at the bar and ordered another drink. It would never happen again. Whatever they could recover would dissipate like smoke the moment he entered the house and fear took over, fear of entanglement, fear of having to repeat forever the anticipation that leads to lust, fear of the habits that couples fall into in order to disguise the loss of desire.

With the aid of the mojitos he was able to reconsider the possibility that he wasn't good enough, that he should give up his writing career in favor of something more lucrative, maybe join his father in the real-estate business or go to law school. As his grandmother told him a few months before she died, You're still young. You can do anything you want. That's what grandmothers always say. After his fifth drink his will wavered and he envisioned his two books, standing at a doorway like forlorn children whose father is about to abandon them.

The next morning Angel was at the nursing home promptly at nine. He found Pedro in his room shaving. He was wearing a pajama top but no bottom. His legs were wrinkled and veiny and his testicles hung midway down his thighs. For a moment Angel saw himself in his place and considered the awful fate that awaited him.

Grandfather, he said, addressing him for the first time in the familial way.

Aren't you a little early? he said looking at Angel through the mirror.

There are a few details I need to know for my story.

I told you all there is. Angel could hear the double razor scratching at the bristles on his neck, going over the scars where the surgeons had gone in.

Some things don't add up, Angel said, having no idea what he was referring to but sensing that Pedro wasn't telling him the whole story.

I don't want to suffocate to death.

What?

I had a dream last night that I was drowning. When I woke I couldn't breathe. I called the nurse and she gave me oxygen.

Angel didn't know at the time, nor did Pedro, that the cancer had spread to his lungs and he was, in effect, drowning in his own fluids.

Today, I want you to take me out to breakfast.

Once he was done shaving Angel helped him with his pants, which he held up with suspenders over a blue long-sleeved shirt.

They drove to a Cuban cafeteria on Calle Ocho whose owner Pedro had known for six decades. The owner sat behind the counter smoking a cigar.

Come in, come in and drink a chair, because the water zero's coming, he said, translating a Cuban phrase into thickly literal English.

Albenio, Pedro said. This is my grandson. He is a famous writer and he's writing a story about me.

Not exactly, Angel wanted to say but he didn't have the opportunity.

Your grandfather, Albenio said, was the best cop in Havana. He caught and killed Manolito Rivas and received a ten-thousand-dollar reward. In those days that was a fortune.

Angel looked at Pedro. It was the first time he'd heard about the reward.

I want fried eggs, bacon, Cuban bread, and café con leche, Pedro said. I'm sick of that shit they feed me in the nursing home.

What about the reward? Angel asked. Grandmother must have been happy about that.

Pedro shrugged his shoulders and ordered a cold beer. That was something Angel had seen his father do, drink beer in the morning.

I bet she was, Albenio said, speaking through a half smile as if he were keeping a secret.

Pedro waited for the beer and drank some of it looking out the window at the traffic going by. He and Albenio spoke of other matters, friends they had in common in Havana, most of them dead or dying—Panchito Cantera, who had owned a car dealership and was now a living corpse; Alberto Torres, the artist, who'd lost his legs to diabetes; Humberto González, who sold pharmaceuticals and had more bypass surgeries than you could count; and others in wheelchairs, on life support systems, bedridden, under the ground—a catalogue of morbidity that made Angel's hair stand on end.

There is Miami, Pedro said. And then there is an underground city where all the old Cubans are buried with their memories and dreams. That is where the real Havana lies. Upside down. One hundred years from now, when all the Cubans are gone, that city too, will disappear.

Unless the memories are written down, Angel said stupidly.

Written memories are ossified memories.

Have you heard the one about the Galician couple whose baby falls out a third-story window? Albenio asked.

A thousand times.

Just then the food arrived. Pedro picked at his eggs and ordered another beer. He was done in fifteen minutes. Albenio refused to accept payment, claiming sixty years of friendship was payment enough.

In the car on the way home Angel asked Pedro again about the reward money. He admitted that Zoila never saw a penny.

What happened to it?

I gave it to Manolito's mother. The only good thing Manolito Rivas ever did was take care of his mother. I killed him. The least I could do was make sure she was provided for.

How about Zoila? Angel said, his temper rising. After his grandfather left her, Zoila suffered one privation after another, living in tenements across Havana and working as a washerwoman and maid for several well-to-do families.

What about her? In the end we all wound up broke and in exile. That's the way things are. Pedro grew pensive and looked out the window.

In the realm of the heartless the generous man is a fool, especially he who gives blindly. Angel understood two things then: First, his grandfather was a generous man; second, his grandfather had been heartless. The two qualities had somehow joined in him and become one, or, better yet, both lived in him simultaneously. Nothing else could be said about that, despite any familial allegiance Angel had for his grandmother and father, who had suffered so much at the hands of this heartless, generous man.

When they got to the nursing home, Angel parked on the front driveway. He went around to the passenger side and helped Pedro walk to the door.

I'll go from here, he said, waving his hand in a way that was both a dismissal and a farewell.

Leaning on his walker he took small shuffling steps to the elevator and waited there until the door opened. He looked quickly in Angel's direction and offered a smile that came from the depths of his misery. Then he disappeared.

THE MAN WITH THE HANDLEBAR MUSTACHE

Two months after meeting her, Angel moved in with Amanda. He was tired of bony females and jagged angles, tired of their clacking as they turned over in bed. He wanted the softness of clouds, the keening of inner organs trapped in flesh, a body like laughter, the breeching of whales in an icy fjord. Amanda wore caftans and heavy silver jewelry on her arms that jangled loudly when she moved. He could hear her in the kitchen, he could hear her in the bathroom, and he could hear her in the hallway outside the door even before he could see her. She was devoted to necromancy and had a gift for communicating with the dead, asking them questions the answers to which came in code. If she asked, Will I be able to pay the rent next month? the answer might be, The effervescence of golf balls afflicts a pretentious entity. Which might mean yes or no depending on the position of the stars at the moment the question was asked and on the amplitude of her imagination, which matched her body's.

When Amanda spoke, underground springs burst from her voice, and when she breathed she blew a hot southern wind that brought with it the nostalgia of tropical forests. She was the best lover Angel ever had. She had no scruples, and the word *no* did not exist for her in bed. Once, after a particular session in which the firmaments blew open and the oceans parted, she told him that his mother had communicated with her and told her the name and address of the man who had knifed him. He laughed, not believing her, in any event, not wanting to know so many years after the incident who it was who had almost caused his demise. Vengeance has its statute of limitations. He nodded and stared at the ceiling, thinking about muse spiders. She added that the attacker had a handlebar mustache and five daughters and lived in their neighborhood. He nodded again and pretended to fall asleep.

What was he supposed to do, find the man, confront him, and seek retribution of some sort? Not worth the effort. He had healed fully, the only evidence of the knifing a small scar on his belly where the blade slipped through. Amanda liked to lick the scar. Like a little worm, she once said, a slimy sugar worm floating on the milk of his belly. He was lucky. It could have been an anvil dropped on his head from a fifth-floor window. It could have been a drunk driver jumping the curb and crushing him against the liquor store. It could have been something less obvious but no less lethal—an aneurism, a massive coronary.

For a long time he wished the knifer would die a horrible death. That wish was still hiding in a recondite part of his mind, but he was no longer willing to act on it. His will had been diverted to other pursuits. So when Amanda told him what his mother had revealed to her, he was upset, not because it brought back that awful night and the months of recovery, but because he was expected—expected himself—to act on the information.

He sat up in bed and said, I won't do it.

Amanda asked, Do what?

Find the man with the mustache and the five daughters. There must be more than one man in this city who wears a handlebar mustache and is the father of five daughters.

Who lives in our neighborhood? Amanda asked.

How do we know you weren't dreaming.

I was dreaming, she said.

How do we know the information is reliable?

It came from your mother, she said.

It could have been a demon in disguise. You've said sometimes demons trick people by assuming the identity of a loved one.

This was no demon. It was your mother.

Are you sure?

Her maiden name was González.

He left the house that morning and walked around the neighborhood reluctantly with the word *retribution* stuck in his head like an iron spike. What is a neighborhood, anyway? Three, four, five blocks? He walked ten and saw no one with a handlebar mustache, except for Isidore, the eighty-year-old former waiter who lived on the sixth floor of their building.

He could have done it, Amanda said.

Isidore is a sweet gay man, Angel said, his exasperation rising, and he walks with a cane.

That day Angel went about his business—he'd promised Amanda he would wash the windows and do the laundry while she attended her necromancy meeting. Nevertheless, the matter stayed with him if for no other reason than to heed his mother's message to find his attacker. He didn't have the faintest idea what he would do once he confronted him. He went to the Tenth Precinct and asked for a copy of the police report, which he read carefully twice. It said nothing he didn't already know, except that given the uneven edges of the wound, the perpetrator most probably used a serrated knife with a one-inch-wide blade. He filed away the paperwork along with other documents relating to that night and went to sleep, too tired to wait up for Amanda.

Waking the next morning he saw that Amanda had slept next to him and then left the house early. On her pillow was a note saying she had gone in search of the man with the handlebar mustache. He dressed quickly and went outside without so much as a cup of coffee. He walked around the neighborhood until he found her staring through the window of a phony French café on Ninth Avenue. All French cafés in Cubop City are phony. The real ones are in France.

That's the man, she said looking through Angel's reflection on the glass.

Inside were several youngish couples seated at the tables closest to the window, and at one of the far tables by the counter was a middle-aged man, alone, reading a book.

What are you talking about? He doesn't have a mustache, he said.

Your mother appeared to me again last night and said that he'd shaved it off. She said that two of his daughters lived in the city, and the three others, whom he'd lost touch with, were spread all over the country.

But how do you know it's that particular man? Angel asked, letting his irritation get the better of him. I'd got over all this and you had to bring my mother into it.

I didn't call her, Amanda said in a calm voice that thinly disguised her condescension. She came to me. I'll tell you how I know that's our man.

Angel threw his arms up over his head and started walking away. His mother was dead. He, his sister, and father had had her cremated and dumped her ashes into the Gulf Stream. Amanda caught up with him and grabbed him by the arm.

You should have seen him handling the butter knife, like a bona fide killer. What I didn't get to say to you because you left so abruptly was that your mother told me we would find him in that café, sitting just where he is.

Amanda, he said almost pleading with her. You never knew my mother.

I know her better than you think. What harm can there be if we follow that man and find out where he lives?

They waited across the street for the man to finish his coffee and watched him as he left the café and walked south on the avenue. He was slim, almost delicate, and had thinning blond hair. He looked to be in his late fifties, hardly the attacker type. They followed him at a safe distance to Twenty-third Street, where he turned east, then to the Eighth Avenue subway, which he entered going uptown.

Hurry, Amanda said. We're about to lose him.

No way, he said.

Amanda said they'd gone too far to stop now and went down the subway steps. He went home. He had windows to wash.

Three hours later she showed up at the apartment, disheveled and sweaty. Subways will do that to you. He watched her as she drank a glass of water, went to the bathroom, and came back to the living room to sit on the sofa. She let out a long breath, closed her eyes, and let her head rest on the back cushion.

He's an actor, she said finally.

He lowered the newspaper he was reading and made a question with his face.

I knew there was something familiar about his face, she said. I thought I had seen it in a dream. Then, as he was getting off the subway on Fifty-ninth Street, he turned toward me and I got a frontal view. It was the guy on the Electrolux commercial on the television. We got the wrong man.

There was nothing Angel could say, nothing at all. Maybe now they could put this whole thing to rest and resume their lives as normal people. They did for a time. Two weeks later as they were having supper at their favorite neighborhood diner, she said in a barely audible register, as if she were trying to keep him from hearing it, We have to start over.

He stopped chewing and looked at her. He could feel his eyes squinting.

Your mother has been appearing to me every night. She's very insistent, you know. The only way to quiet her is to find the man with the handlebar mustache.

He grew it back? Angel asked.

He never shaved it. I misinterpreted some symbols.

He took another bite of his turkey club sandwich and at that moment an important question occurred to him. His mother could barely speak English when she was alive and Amanda's Spanish was rudimentary at best. What language were they communicating in? How do you say *handlebar* in Spanish? Or is that not a relevant question in the spirit world? He kept these matters to himself and continued eating. A few minutes later he felt a kick to his shin, which he ignored. He felt it again. Amanda was pointing behind him and raising her eyebrows. He turned around, trying his best to be discreet, and a few tables away was a man with a handlebar mustache. He was dark haired and muscular. His face was long and bony and his cheeks were covered with acne scars. There was something hard about him, something criminal.

Angel couldn't finish his sandwich. Suddenly he wanted to be out of the diner, safe at home watching baseball, his favorite pastime in those days. Amanda was scrunched in her seat, hiding behind him as she spied the man, who had by now noticed he was being watched.

Slowly the man with the handlebar mustache stood and walked over to their table, all six and a half feet of him. He loomed over them and squinted amorally like Lee Van Cleef looking into a western vastness. A cold liquid ran through Angel's veins, and he readied himself to protect Amanda, perform the ultimate sacrifice for honor's sake, and be torn asunder by this Chelsea desperado.

Amanda smiled up at him. She had a knowing, innocent smile that would disarm the most determined killer—yes, even Lee himself at his meanest.

Are you Rollie Fingers? she asked him.

Bless her, Angel thought. Bless women who know baseball.

The Chelsea desperado's meanness dissolved and he showed them a set of nicotine-stained teeth. Sweetheart, you got the wrong jockey.

For quite a while Amanda busied herself with other things and dropped the matter. He was liberated and was able to concentrate on his work, which he'd neglected in order to pursue the handlebar chimera. It was around this time that he began to feel a twinge in his belly, not pain exactly, but what Spanish speakers call una penita, a small sorrow. He ignored it, as one does with such things, hoping it would go away by itself, but one night the pain was piercing enough that it woke him. He sat upright in bed sweating and still in the thrall of a dream in which it was not a knife that was thrust into him but a hot poker that twisted itself around his intestines. He shook Amanda awake and told her about the pain but not the dream. She called the surgeon who took care of him the first time, and he urged them to go to the emergency room.

While they waited for the surgeon Amanda said the recurrence of the pain was a wake-up call. Now he had to find the attacker for sure or he would suffer forever. Angel was on intravenous morphine at the time, floating in a plane where everything made sense, or nothing made sense but it was too much trouble to unravel it: a skein of cause and consequence. Morphine takes you to the edge, and it's amazing how clear things are from there. He looked at Amanda and saw concern shadowing her face. He wanted to kiss her. He couldn't remember if he already had. He was absolutely certain he could fly and she could fly with him. He remembered the doctor coming. He remembered a CAT scan, blood tests, X-rays. He remembered the doctor saying he had an abscess—fairly common in these cases—that he would have to drain. He remembered nodding out, a tube in his stomach, nasty nurses and nice nurses, a spot of blood that seeped onto the sheets, the fellow next to him whose stomach had been taken out. He hadn't eaten in three weeks. His eyes were sunken and his lips were gray. According to Amanda, he'd be dead soon. His aura was diminishing.

While Angel was home recovering, he asked Amanda what language she and his mother used to communicate. No language, she said. What do you mean? he asked. The spirit world is beyond language, she said. We use signs and and we use thoughts. He dropped the subject and fell asleep on the sofa. He dreamed of a river on which words floated and sank and floated again. He dreamed of being dizzy with loneliness. Finally he dreamed of the man who knifed him, who lived in his neighborhood and was waiting for the right moment to knife him again, this time aiming better and deeper so that he would die miserably on the dirty chewing-gum-splattered sidewalk.

Angel survived the abscess without complications or need of major surgery, due in no small measure to the surgeon who treated him, one of the best in the city, and he went on about his life as if he'd never been knifed. Few cities allow for that sort of continuation and Cubop City is one. Then he received a call from a detective in the Tenth Precinct. They had a suspect in hand and wanted him to identify the perpetrator that same afternoon. He and Amanda rushed to the station house, and, as the six suspects were lined up before them, she grabbed his hand and pressed it. One of the men had a handlebar mustache. He asked the detective, who was sitting next to them, if the man lived in their neighborhood, and he nodded his head yes. Police procedure prevented him from answering out loud. I think that's him, he said. You sure of that? the detective asked. Angel could sense Amanda's eyes boring into him. Yes, he said.

After that it was only a matter of time. He testified at the trial a year later. The man had by now shaved off his mustache but it didn't matter. He identified him and the court-appointed defense lawyer offered a weak and ineffectual cross-examination. He was found guilty. Then the judge discovered some inconsistencies in the prosecutor's papers and the case was thrown out. The man was let go. Justice had been done. Amanda wasn't so sure.

She tried contacting Angel's mother again on several occasions but she was unsuccessful. Her necromancy mentor told her that once the dead accomplish their goal they disappear forever. She's joined the ether, the tutor said. She won't hear you or see you, nor can you see or hear her. The best you can do is breathe in and breathe out and hope that a molecule or two that were once part of her is in the air. Let it in, the tutor added, let it all in. In physics lies redemption.

YOU SAY BEAUTY

It is a special night. You have left a party held in your honor in a big house once owned by the niece of a Philadelphia banking magnate. Mainline Brahmins used to visit the house, invited by the niece to spend a weekend in the country, away from the bustle of their urban lives. Now, after passing through several owners, the house is being rented by a group of artists who do many more drugs than art. The house is falling apart, its ghosts long gone, but the artists don't care. They paint a few pictures or make believe they paint, then down the LSD, snort the cocaine, smoke the weed. There are many people at the party, most of whom you find unpleasant. The men are scraggly and bearded, the women thin and unwashed. They have come not because of art but because of the liquor and the drugs. An hour ago the wife of a truck driver offered herself to you in the attic and after the sex you wanted to get away from her. Her armpits were unshaven, a fact that you noticed in the postcoitus. She talked too much but said nothing. Nights are like that. Desire in, desire out. You say beauty and everything crumbles. You will make meaning out of this many years hence. Now her husband, the truck driver, wants to show a pornographic movie in the living room. Perhaps he knows about the sex upstairs. All you want to do is go outside, get away from the wife, the husband, the film. Nothing personal. A soft breeze blows in from the south and you can hear a loon in the distance, sounding serene and plaintive at once, where the bad music doesn't reach.

There's a small wooden rowboat tied to the dock and you take it out to the middle of the river, where the moon is waiting for you. On both banks there are large shadowy trees and beyond them the crumbling estates where the wealthy once gamboled. The moon looms under you, big, white and pock marked. You bend over the edge of the rowboat to kiss it, aiming for the Sea of Tranquillity, but you would much prefer the dark side if you could reach it. You like the unknown, the unseen, the black kiss. Inches away from the surface you recognize the smells of benzene and untreated sewage floating over the sweet scent of decomposing leafy matter. It is not the river of your dreams, of your wanting, no matter how much you've drunk tonight. Still, it is the only river you've got.

Moments before your lips meet the water, too late now to go back on your intent, you tip over and fall through the surface, disappearing into the brown depths and leaving behind a string of pearly bubbles that pop softly on the surface. That's the way it always is. Glub-glub but no one listens, glub-glub where the river is the same, never the same, and the moon awaits your undoing.

THE MAGNIFICENT (M)OTHERS

First there was Tata, black Earth Mother who coddled him like his real mother never could. As a small boy Angel wanted to sink into her and disappear forever into her loving, unconditional and absolute like the ocean that surrounded him on all sides. He remembers—he thinks he remembers— her huge breasts, against which he leaned when he sat on her lap, and her soft hands the color of loam as they moved over him in the bath. In the fog of early memories there were games—she touched here, he touched there—and squirms of joy. Laughter like shallow water, like waves, broke over them. She taught him to love the night, which was in her, like the sea creature that comes in his dreams and beaches where his heart beats. Her real name was sacred, therefore secret, and so he learned never to reveal it.

In the first grade he and a girl named Lilian would sit together during recess and relate to each other what member of their respective families they had seen naked the day before. I saw my mother, he'd say. I saw my father, she'd respond. I saw my sister. I saw my uncle. I saw my third cousin. She's fifteen years old and has nipples like chocolate kisses. I saw the gardener peeing. His pee-pee's like a yellow hose. Like a banana. Like a chunk of yuca! I saw the maid after she took a bath. Her pendejera was thick as a jungle and it was dripping wet. The testimonials were only as detailed as seven-year-olds could make them, and whatever physiological taxonomy they lacked was offset by rich metaphorical references that delight him now whenever he enters the country of the past. After their exchanges deteriorated into vulgar catalogues of fleshy parts, he started elaborating—her breasts are like balls of cheese; his pee-pee is the size of El Morro Castle when it stands up.

In the fourth grade, he, a girl named Miriam, and his friend Oscar had to stay in the classroom during recess for talking in class. After the teacher warned them they were not to talk among themselves, she said, It's a beautiful day, and went out to catch her breath and smoke a cigarette. While she was gone, in silent glee and without exchanging a word, the three of them went to the blackboard and drew huge penises entering equally huge vaginas in a sort of scholastic cavern-painting orgy. They erased the drawings when the bell rang.

By the water fountain, a girl whose name he never learned asked him if he wanted to see su cosita. It would cost him a real, ten cents. He looked at her fingers. They were white and puffy. She was American, from the state of Kentucky. The nails were pink and culminated in white slivers of moon. Only then did he notice her red hair and freckled face. Of course he paid the price. He keeps paying it, even now when his memories are copies of his memories and the original is lost under many layers of remembering.

Sunning herself on the beach of his making is his cousin, Martica. She was a plain girl, thin and bony. Through her face skittered the permanent scowl of disenchantment. She appeared, even to an eight-year-old with limited experience, moody and irksome, and she had to be handled as one handles a sea urchin. Angel had been invited to spend the day at the beach by Martica's mother, Ada. He dreaded the idea. He was not keen on sitting on the sand in the middle of the day, certainly not with his boring cousin and officious aunt, but his mother insisted he go. It would do him good, she'd said, to swim in the ocean, splash around in the waves, play with children his own age. He hated children his age.

Angel sat on the edge of the beach blanket watching a group of children chasing the waves, hoping they wouldn't ask him to join them, when he lowered his eyes and came upon Martica's feet. Her toes were perfectly proportioned, her middle and third slightly longer than her big toe and gently curved, as if in response to the arch, which was a marvel of skeletal architecture, parabolic and fleshy, yet not so pronounced as to break completely with the line of the heel. Oh, he was transfixed, he was smitten. A surge of fluids within him quickened his heart and made the small bud between his legs stand straight away from his body. From that day on he became an adorer of feet.

Samara, whose father was an important functionary in the Communist Party, winked at him in math class. She assumed that superior attitude of someone who believes hers is the only truth. Her feet were glorious appendages, of the sort that, when he was older, would make him swoon. He saw them once, at the school's annual swim party and barbecue. He remembers them now as patrician and high arched, with toes like minnows—not at all the proletarian feet one would expect, given her family's political inclinations. Her behavior was colored by ambivalence born of equanimity. To this day he does not know what that wink in math class meant, everything or nothing. Samara, that little Marxist, stands forever in his mind's eye and ear, singing "The Internacionale."

Not long after that, Martica and her family left for the United States. His family left a year later and he was not to see her again for many years. Over time, by dint of careful observation coupled with the focus of someone seeking, beyond all other ambition, perfection lost, he grew to acquire an extraordinary knowledge of the female foot. As a teenager he looked through newspapers and magazines in search of advertisements for shoes or stockings. Best were nail-polish ads, for they showed the whole foot and featured the toes, those unparalleled glories of the human anatomy that filled his body with hormonal explosions. The onanistic flights he went on with those photographs, however, were nothing compared to the ecstasies of longing he experienced in contemplation of the real feet he saw naked on the beach or clad in sandals on city streets in summertime.

When he entered the university, he braved the dangerous streets of the red-light district. There he consorted with prostitutes who showed him their extremities for a fee. Of all he saw and touched and reveled over, none was as well formed as Martica's. Soon he ran out of money and concluded he might have better luck with regular women. He went out with dozens and became serious with those few who considered as a matter of course his habit of looking at and caressing their feet and who enjoyed the novel way in which his lips sucked and his tongue curled around their toes.

Olga, dark-haired queen of the dance floor, played him like a yo-yo. Her curvaceous and free-flowing body more than made up for her flat, undistinguished feet. She made him do the dog walk, the high-wire act, the loop around the world. All the tugging and pulling made him dizzy. Older, more experienced than he, she taught him many things, most important, that without being vulnerable one cannot entertain mystery, the most profound of which, after death, is love. When she ran off with the singer of a rock band, he felt as if someone had punched him in the stomach. He still feels it sometimes when it rains. His Jesuit teachers had been priming him to enter the order, but after Olga, St. Ignatius didn't stand a chance. He recently found her letters in an old trunk filled with papers and was surprised at how maudlin love can be from a distance.

The singularities of life and the accidents of circumstance led him to Irene, the black-Irish girl who was taller than he by three inches. Toes splaying in all directions, her feet were batrachian, of the sort that stick to walls and ceilings. Her humor, which was sharp and furious, saved her. No one, not pundits, priests, or proselytes, escaped the poison darts that flew from her mouth. With him she was careful and made sure that the barbs that came in his direction were lined with felt. Reluctant to have sex, she finally succumbed in the family room of her parents' Scarsdale home.

Berta, from the Dominican Republic, was sexual and insatiable with smooth cinnamon skin and smart luminous eyes. They went many places together but always wound up in bed when the day was done. He didn't ask many questions, nor did she. There was something about the way she moved up and down his body, something about her smell and her taste that made him think of redemption. Berta pushed him deeper in. It was the end of the sixties. He'd been in the United States not quite ten years. Life was a cabaret, life was a Lucumí chant, life was ten tons of metal on the back of a dump truck headed east on the BQE. Domesticity led him to drown in the ocean of his obsession. He could never have enough of Berta. So he left. Crawled out of the muck and moved to the suburbs, which offered a dullness he confused for peace of mind.

Vanessa used to sing boleros before she met him. Afterward, she didn't sing a note but mumbled incoherencies while the adorer of feet sat in rapt contemplation of hers. They were calloused and bunioned with corns growing on all her toes, which were very beautiful but smelled like rotten cheese. After hearing him whimper on the rug by their bed, she grew ashamed and wrapped her extremities in burlap, which did not help her infections but did wonders for her self-esteem. She sang him a final bolero and told him, Eres un enfermo, vete a la pinga—two Cuban expressions that can communicate many things but in this particular case meant he should get as far away from her as he possibly could.

The succession of women that followed was notable because of their sameness. There was Amber, Eloisa, Sandra, and Susana, whom he married for her mind, a deadly mistake; Anne, whom he also married and with whom he had two daughters. There was Olympia, who was, in contrast to her name, petite; two Nancies; and one Michelle, dull and viscous and feral. They were all the same to him, devoid of individuality and, therefore, in the end, boring. No more poring over podiatry textbooks, no more hours wasted surfing the Internet.

He grew despondent and was without a woman for eighteen months. His hands began shaking at odd moments, and he woke at night in cold sweats, which could only be cured by drinking substantial amounts of alcohol. He suffered stomach ailments and muscle cramps; his temples grew gray, his voice weak and distorted; yet, despite the maladies, his writing acquired an acumen it never had before. As a result he began publishing his work with regularity and he received invitations from many universities to lecture and read his fiction.

Angel heard from relatives that Martica had married an Albanian building superintendent and moved to a far-off borough of Cubop City. Imagine his surprise and delight! He called Martica and went to see her that same afternoon. On the long subway ride out he sang and laughed to himself and gave money to three different panhandlers, only one of whom seemed in dire need.

When they saw each other he and Martica embraced. He pulled her to arms' length and saw that she had filled out and was not as unattractive as he imagined. Life had done interesting things to her face. Beside himself with anxiety and disregarding any sense of decorum, he confessed to her that he had become enthralled with her feet. He exaggerated and said that every waking hour since they had last seen each other he had thought about them, keeping them alive in the fire of his memory until such time as he found a like pair to replace them. But he hadn't.

She was shocked and brought her hand to her mouth, where it rested obliquely. She was about to walk away when she realized his anguish and offered a smile. She pointed down and there at the end of her legs was a pair of brown orthopedic shoes, tied on the side, that looked like two loaves of rustic Albanian bread.

My feet, she said, have been the source of much pain over the years. I've had many surgeries. They are mutilated beyond recognition. I wouldn't show them to anyone.

On the inside he swooned and almost fell into a maelstrom of despair. On the outside he was kind and familiar. He kissed her again on the forehead and left her apartment as soon as prudence allowed. He never got to meet her Albanian husband, never got to see her again. In his mind Martica was dead and her feet had gone to hell.

ORGIES

Have you ever participated in an orgy? Amanda asked him two weeks after they met.

No, Angel answered, resisting the temptation to lie. By previous agreement the postcoitus tolerated only total honesty. Have you?

Not quite.

What does that mean? You either have or you haven't.

He was lying in bed with his eyes closed and the covers up to his chest and wanted very much to sleep, but he fought the urge in order to hear about Amanda's experience.

It happened last summer when Sandy and I were in Naples.

Sandy was Amanda's best friend from childhood. They were on a European trip, paid for by Amanda's parents as a graduation gift. Angel had met Sandy once in passing and had briefly entertained the fantasy of being in bed with the two of them, a satyr with two nubile nymphs whose combined age was forty-two. Picasso of the written word! The thought pleased him enormously. He was convinced he could satisfy two young women at the same time.

Sandy met two Italians on the street and came home with them, Amanda said. The three of them were drunk. Gino and Paolo. I think they were lovers. Sandy had a plastic container with a roast chicken inside. She carried it under her arm like a football. Dinner, she announced, and lifted the chicken over her head. The boys brought wine, which we drank straight out of the bottle. I turned on a small radio I'd brought with me and we danced. Then we took off our clothes.

Amanda got out of bed and went to the bathroom. When she came back his eyes were open again and he'd lost all desire to sleep.

So?

So Sandy is really looped by now and she starts dancing around the room by herself, chewing on a piece of chicken. Gino was smoking a cigarette and laughing at her. Paolo was sitting next to me on the couch getting increasingly annoyed, his erection drooping to the right. Finally Sandy plopped down on the easy chair and passed out with chicken fat all over her face and the half-eaten chicken leg on her belly. The two Italian boys got dressed and left.

Is that it? he said bolting up in bed. He wanted so much more. It felt like a truncated dream.

I told you it was an almost orgy. Nothing came of it.

Do you still want to be in one?

Only with the right people. Those boys were strange. So is Sandy, but I knew that all along. Do you?

Do I what?

Do you want to be in an orgy?

What defines an orgy?

Four or more people, Amanda said with a superior tone that annoyed him. He felt the urge to go to the bathroom but he didn't want the conversation to stop.

Too many for me. How about three people?

That's a ménage à trois. Two women or two men?

He felt offended that she should even ask. Two women, of course.

You old goat! she said, giggling.

Don't you think I can handle two?

I have no doubt. You've handled me and I'm worth at least two.

Now he really had to go. He rushed out of bed and stood over the toilet forcing out the pee, not like the old days when he urinated with the exuberance of a stallion. As he pushed out the last few spurts he looked at himself in the mirror that lined the wall. He could do it, no? Go on a romp with Amanda and Sandy? It would be good for his prostate if nothing else. Not a young stallion, he, but an old goat about to pipe his ultimate tune. He flushed, turned off the light, and went back into bed where Amanda lay, softly sleeping.

BIG BABEL

Paralyzed some days. Other days you waited for the bus and others still you trembled like a deer caught in the headlights of the dump truck of language. Quizás no tenga amor la eternidad. That old bolero. Eternity, however, doesn't wait for anyone. Eternity has nothing to do with language. Standing in midtown Cubop City you tried to unravel yourself from the skein—Spanish, English, or both, each thread leading back into itself. The light turned many colors and you were kept from crossing the street and going where you had to go. It got quite hot. Anonymous, odorous hordes passed by you, and you, too, were anonymous, sweaty.

A man, quite possibly from the Southern Cone, asked you with great difficulty, in an English so broken it sounded like a lost tongue, how to get to the East Village. You affected the posture of the lost, for you, too, were that, though in a different way, and answered him in English, but with a Slavic accent, to walk down Broadway all the way to big park that calls itself Union Squares. To south and east all being East Willage. Large Sicilian place in the old days around Ninth Street and First Avenue, and around Sixth Street and Third, big Ukrainian. Not now so much anymore at present, but big weirdo area and teenager tattoo people from Jersey with needles in noses. Too expensive to live there no more for regular people who speak in other tongues. Queens is good—Astoria, Sunnyside, that's where everybody goes, except old ladies in babushkas. Shit, they wear black stockings and pee in their panties. Russkies living in Brighton Beach by the sea, like Odessa. I got relatives there, drive limo. Blacks in Harlem or in jail. Puerto Ricans in the Bronx, Dominicans in Washington Heights—Quisqueya—and the Colombians in Flushing, around there. The Medellín cartel, the cocaine, that kinds of things. Indians all over the place and Jamaican nurses in hospital and the Chinese delivery boys and the Mexican dishwashers. All the rich people live on Park Avenue and the Jews on Long Island. Liberals in the Upper West Side. They make to believe they like the aliens, but in their secret they wish everyone to be like them with Birkenstocks and beards. They no patient. Cubop City big Babel, big bagel, big apple. Take a bite. Ha ha.

The man was more lost now, and over his face came a pained look, as if he would never find the East Village. He wished he were back in Asunción, you were sure, but you wouldn't give him the satisfaction of speaking Spanish to him, which you could easily have done, and put him at ease a little bit. No, señor. You were not in Midtown, intralanguage paraly-sis, to make anyone feel comfortable, least of all yourself. That is not what Cubop City is about. You want comfort, you go to Terre Haute, Indiana. Cubop City is about feeling foreign all the time and staying awake nights wondering where your language went and where your grandparents are from and why you feel so different from everyone else that walks past you on the street. Like that little guy from Montevideo, who was desperately trying to find his way to the East Village. Why did he want to go there, anyway?

That night you couldn't sleep. You tossed this way, that way. You drank three glasses of water, then had to void your blad-der as many times. You thought you should make it up to the fellow from the Southern Cone, but how? You had no name, no address. You didn't even know what country he was from. All you had was a face contorted by anxiety and the question, Güer to Iss Billage? compounded by your own unwillingness to speak to him in his language, which was your language. You'd never done such a thing before. According to psychology, at the core of human behavior is the trauma of birth and infancy and your parents' trauma and their parents' trauma. The sins of the parents shall be visited upon the children. Actually, that's the Old Testament, but then Freud was an Old Testament kind of guy. What sin of your parents was now rearing up like a ball-peen hammer about to strike?

It all went back to language. You had two at your disposal the day the man from the Southern Cone came to you seek-ing succor. You decided to use a disguised form of English and throw the poor man off track, as if he weren't off enough already. You left him wondering what planet of the solar system he had just landed on. It had nothing to do with early childhood trauma, nothing to do with your parents' suffering. It was the fear of revealing yourself. As you say this, you tremble and your stomach churns. Language is your mask to fashion at will, from native-born Cuban to foreign-born Slav—Ruthenian, to be exact. You fooled that man into thinking you a creature quite unlike you are. You are master of your identity, not he who made the mistake of asking you a simple directional question. He may as well have asked where paradise lay. The answer came as layered as a mil hojas cake. Only in Cubop City. Only in yourself.

In the morning you walked out the building a little lighter, your heart a little cleaner. You went west with the warmth of the sun at your back. This neighborhood now often feels like the city twenty years ago before all the hipness began to invade it: old-fashioned coffee shops, bagel stores, greasy Chinese takeouts, a dry cleaner and a cobbler next to each other, several Irish bars within a couple of blocks. You know it well. Some days you feel like you're going to drown in the backwardness, the lack of nouvelle cuisine and smart people sitting at sidewalk restaurants, but today, today is different. You're in disguise, and you know it, and all around you, the old ladies creeping along hunched over their aluminum walkers, the butcher and the fishmonger and the cop and the optometrist and the ditchdigger and the young woman in high boots and sunglasses waving for a taxi and the fellow pissing against the wire fence of the school, everyone's in disguise, passing one another, avoiding one another's eyes, until the moment comes when someone stops you for directions and then the disguise is in danger of falling away. You react quickly, spontaneously, and hold it up, change it if need be in order to deflect the stranger's attempt at communication. I Slav, you say, I Ruthenian from Carpathian Mounten, and you stop the man dead in his tracks.

The morning was dim city light falling on the streets full of people: grand dames of Cubop City, politicians, drivers of armored trucks, cooks and waiters and tax collectors and yoga teachers and stripteasers and Goth teenagers, and you, bilingual loafer among them. Who could imagine such fortune? Who wouldn't give everything he owns to be in your sneakers, central and ubiquitous, denuded and invisible, omnivalent, fractal, momentary, copacetic?

AMATORY PURSUIT

But this is Amanda's story. She's the one for whom the daily bread rises in the oven and the waterfalls sing on the rocks and the clouds pass by morphing into the creatures of dreams. She's the one. Ask anyone who knows her; ask the sands that spread from the ocean to her house; ask the house as it listens to the waves sliding up on shore, crying, Amanda, Amanda; and the sun at dusk like a big mouth sucking up the light; and the labyrinth of Amanda's heart that no one yet has broken; and the minotaur inside the labyrinth that awaits those foolish enough to enter. It bellows through the night and paws the ground when it hears the wind rushing through the infinite chambers.

Angel met Amanda before she took up hammering and before she learned about Christian colonics. Everything was gray and dirty. Dog feces with bottle-fly mountain climbers lay on the sidewalk, Styrofoam cups like white Turcoman fezzes plugged the sewers, the subways roared and clanged, half-eaten slices of pizza stewed in the summer sun, and garbage overflowed on all the corners of the city, where it was flattened by the passersby and smashed into postindustrial paste. He was watching the end of the world on television, he was bathing in a tub filled with the tepid water of serenity, he was reading a book about the musculature of giraffe tongues, he was being an Ur-realist and consorting with oopy-poopy frumpy academics. She came into the room and her eyes fixed on him. Quiet, unprepossessing, young, she sat among the tweedy toads, the chokers of metaphysical swans, and absorbed all the light in the room. It was her eyes he couldn't let go of, her eyes that wouldn't let go of him. He lost his thought and let it run away into the highest pinnacle of intellectual obfuscation. He gagged. Nothing meant anything anymore except for that young woman who walked out of the room as obtrusively as she had entered. Was she bored, disinterested? Who wouldn't be, listening to the harrumphing intellectuals of the new millennium? But now: The room was an airplane crash, the city was spinning out of control, the world was fleeing into a cosmic soup of mystery, death, and desire. He forsook his role among the postmodernist flatulents and ran after her, but she had disappeared into the crowds that filled the streets with their terrorized silence. Afterward, when the crowds had thinned, he searched for her up and down avenues and alleyways. His life had changed and he couldn't reach the agent of that change to thank her, to curse her.

It was months before he saw Amanda again. By then her hair was long and fell wildly on her shoulders. She wore flowing robes made of rose petals. No, that is not true. She was wearing a long paisley skirt and army boots and the same confident expression. He ran into her in the elevator of an academic institution. She knew his name. He didn't know hers. Ur-realist that he was, he asked for it, though in reality names mean nothing. The inkling in his heart mattered more than the answer to his question in the eyes of a young Terpsichore who would teach him, old essential-ist, the indigos and scarlets of pleasure, the twists and turns of the dance of romance. She gave it nonetheless, calmly, surely, with a voice that matched her eyes. *Venit, vidit, vicit.* She came, she saw, she conquered, he thought then in his most rudimentary Latin. And the thought led to fear and the fear to a tentativeness he regrets most of all now that he has lost her.

He asked if she might share coffee with him. It was a strange way of saying it, he thinks now. Coffee is the last thing one thinks to share. She said yes, keeping her eyes on his. Blue ice, blue ice on fire is what they were. His heart jumped. They talked. He doesn't remember what about. Let's assume they spoke of literature and writing, their common interests; no, their common obsessions, as it turned out.

She'd read more than most graduate students he knew. They drank coffee and time passed, hours perhaps. It was cen-turies between them, but all time comes to an end, as this did. On parting he imagined himself darkening. His mouth opened into a smile as a wave opens when it breaks. He kissed her on the cheek and let his lips linger there a moment. It was night. On street corners, funky toothless angels sang to him as he passed, jiggling their coins.

SALAO

The underlying hum of construction, the spires, the bridges, the sweetshops, the concrete and glass rising into the slate gray sky, the jackhammers drilling into the street. From above, Cubop City spreads like metal filings out from a magnetic center one may call the heart, but it is more like the liver through which all toxins pass.

There are days when you think the city sucks into itself all who come into it, spitting out bones and clothes. People walk in knowledge of this, in summer heat, cross-town to the East River, and when that offers no relief, back to the West Side and the Hudson. They live in all manner of ways, some in high-rises that almost touch the sky; others, like you, live in tight, airless spaces in which the only way to know the weather is to watch it on television, the only source of comfort in summer

96

an air-conditioning unit that has never worked right. A crazy man who speaks in tongues often stands by your bedroom window at four in the morning and you have to shoo him away. He hurls obscenities at you, sticks out his tongue, long and lascivious, and, after some time, ambles down the street.

If you're a salao like him, you live sprawled on the street under whatever shade the buildings provide. Next to you is a grocery cart packed with your possessions—an old down coat with a ripped sleeve through which feathers escape, an extra pair of pants you haven't worn since last winter because they are too tight around the waist; many, many plastic bags from the different stores of the city; one old wingtip shoe, which you insist on keeping in the hopes that you'll find a matching one; several books you haven't opened since you found them on the curb outside a building in Loisaida; two cans of tunafish; and a transistor radio that gets only one station. On especially hot days you can smell yourself and this causes you great consternation. You'd give anything to take a shower, let the water run over your grime-encrusted body, wash your hair, comb it back like you did when you were still hoping better things would come your way. Hope? Hah!

Salao. That's what you are. You wish the passersby would be quieter, less willing to chatter nonsense or scream at each other from across the street or get into fights when you're trying to sleep; you wish you had more space, a newer air conditioner; you wish language fitted you like stockings. It is loose and unwieldy and makes you mum when you should speak, makes you the butt of jokes told by young lanky men in T-shirts who think they own the world. Lucky they, who have never known what it is to be cursed with the salt of bad fortune; lucky they, who banter and laugh as they walk down the street to the bars on the avenue, where they'll pick up men or women, drink till they're numb, forestall the passage of time, the slow roll downhill, by fucking through the night.

These young people will leave, go back home to Kansas or Indiana, or else marry and move to Massapequa. The salaos remain. Ask the Chinese delivery boy with the bad cough in the freezing rain; ask the Mexican man who arranges flowers outside the Korean deli 24-7; ask the Cuban with his placard denouncing the myriad conspiracies of communism. Ask yourself as you turn on the television to check the weather. The weatherman predicts rain, a cold wind. You take out the little black umbrella you bought for three dollars from the Senegalese vendor on Fourteenth and Fifth. You put on your Yankee hat and a Windbreaker and your waterproof leather boots. You walk outside into the shining sun, the hot gritty air.

THE DEVIL'S SPITE

Next time I saw him he was seated on a bench in Tompkins Square Park. His mustache had turned a yellowish white, and old age had endowed him with a supernatural clairvoyance.

Hammers, he said, hammers and saws. I sensed you coming since yesterday at 3 PM.

Yesterday at three I had no idea that I would be walking by this spot. My plans were to be at my desk writing. I tainted the day that way and called Amanda, who suggested I put aside the writing and go to a movie, trace the outlines of continents on the map, palpate my way out of stasis into the lapidary process of discovery. In other words, Don't call again. Leave me alone.

I tried many things and only walking sufficed. I went to the uptown edges of the island, where the waters of two rivers met and fought each other. I looked down from the Palisades across to Marble Hill and Spuyten Duyvil. As a boy I'd cross the railroad tracks and jump into those waters fully clothed. The game my friends and I played was to avoid the condoms, dead rats, and feces that floated downriver as we swam and came back to the breakwater untouched by the city's effluvia. Last I heard two of them had AIDS, scourge of city pleasures, city life. The others have gone their way speaking a language I no longer care to understand. If they feel the way I do, they have no ambition to see me. One, who liked bridges, may be an engineer; another, who liked animals, may be a veterinarian; the third, who attended Mass daily, a priest; and the youngest, oh, the youngest. He liked nothing, had no ambition, went off to war at eighteen, and returned with half a face and a heroin addiction. Bones, he must be beautiful bones now. He's won the race, left all of us in the dust, and saved himself a lot of time.

The day passed in a thicket of thought, lost passion, youthful dreams diverted, crushed. That night I slept poorly. The next day the computer screen remained blank. I went out and walked in the opposite direction and found myself there in that spot, before the man with handlebar mustache. He recognized me first, since he'd been waiting for me. I sat next to him, disregarding the dried-out pigeon droppings on the wooden slabs of the bench.

Why did you do it? I asked.

He said some nonsense.

I grabbed his arm, which I could have snapped as easily as a dry twig. I tried to explain to him that I could have forgotten the event, forgiven him long ago had he simply disappeared. But he insisted on showing up, tormenting me with sudden appearances, and bringing back the moment of the knifing. This time he did not smile like a rabbit. He looked up at the trees, which were beginning to sprout greenery. I sensed another interpretation.

Some things are done without reason, he said. Some things, if you look deeply at them, shimmer with mystery.

You knifed me, you son of a bitch.

I was done with the subterfuge. That is all I had gotten from this man. And now, without a woman, without a future, I would die alone, in a first-floor walk-down four-hundred-square-foot cave in Chelsea, where no one, not the Korean grocer at the corner or the Indian owner of the liquor store or Frank, who sat outside all day smoking Tiparillos or the actor on the fourth floor who still hoped to make it big or the lady who walked her two pugs on a grocery cart permanently borrowed from Gristedes would care if I lived or died or sought revenge or forgot all about my knifing.

All that matters, Handlebar continued, is not memory or desire, is not hope or despair, or happiness or misery but the fact that you, who were once victim of chance, and I, victimizer of chance, continue to cross paths. The devil's spite? Think that if you wish. The hammers and saws of fate is what I hear. They condone all actions; they turn evil to good and good to evil in an instant. I remember you as a function of something I did at night before a liquor store, unlike you who remember the act as a function of you. If you forget me you will never forgive me; if you forgive, you will never forget.

I stood and looked down at him. The man was a loon. I became convinced he was not the one who knifed me. Perhaps on the next block I would find the antidote against the hammers and saws of fate.

THE ARCHITECTURE
OF PRINCES

Belles lettres. Juan Antonio loved beautiful letters so intensely that sometimes, after reading a story by Nabokov or the prose of Henry James or a passage from Proust, he had an urge to run down the hallways of the university and proclaim in a loud voice that they, not crass Hemingway or boozy Fitzgerald or redneck Faulkner, were the pinnacles of modernity. Borges came close, but his late fictions took a distasteful turn toward violent plots and lowbrow themes. Women writers he considered not worth the mental effort, except Jane Austen and the Brontë sisters, but they were from a century that was veritably owned by the crackpot French, not the petticoated English.

Juan Antonio liked to dress in dark suits with light shirts and brightly colored bow ties. When a lighter mood struck, which was not often, he'd wear light gray worsteds or, in the warm months, olive poplin suits that were popular in the 1970s. If there was the merest chance of rain he carried a bumbershoot, which is what he liked to call his umbrella, thinking that it was an English term, and which he used primarily in the British style as a walking stick.

The short version of his name, Juan Pérez, caused him consternation, for it was as common in Spanish as John Smith is in English. Instead of changing it, he adorned it by adding his second name and surname so that the plaque outside his office door read, Juan Antonio Pérez Ibargoitía, PhD, Comparative Literature. Granted, the Basque name was cumbersome in English, and hardly anyone in the institution, limited by the rigidity of their Anglo-Saxon tongues, knew how to pronounce it. One in particular, a rustic fellow from Alabama, mangled the name so terribly that he took to calling him Ibby for short, a moniker that, to Juan Antonio's dismay, soon caught on in the department among faculty and students alike. Everywhere he went, every door he passed, that silly name was hurled at him, almost as a barb it seemed at times. Hello, Ibby. Ibby, can I talk to you? Juan Antonio swallowed hard and thought it below his dignity to correct them, and so he consoled himself that a nickname was the price one paid for living in a democracy. He was Ibby, or Dr. Ibby to the secretaries in the department office.

Then the new hire showed up. In his midtwenties, he was thin as a rail and wore torn jeans and black high-top sneakers. The department head was beyond herself with glee at having stolen a brilliant prodigy from Princeton who had published a book on the intertextual underpinnings in the work of an obscure Paraguayan novelist. Juan Antonio ignored the young theorist until one day when they met face-to-face in the mail room and the theorist said, Hey Ib, how you doin'? Juan Antonio stopped breathing and felt the muscles of his shoulders tense up. He slowly lifted his eyes until they met the wild matt of hair that sat atop the young man's head.

Hello, Dr. Spellman. How are you finding our department?

Much like any other, Ib. Lots of bullshit, little substance.

Juan Antonio rolled his eyes, but he was nothing if not discreet. He allowed his lips to thin out into a smile, took his leave, and went back to his office, where he seethed with anger. Ib! he thought in disgust. It was only a matter of time before his second surname would disappear altogether and he'd be left with his father's lowly Pérez, which the North Americans would mispronounce anyway, stressing the final syllable, Israeli-style, merely to annoy him. Barbarians, that's what they were. Unwashed barbarians. He packed his leather briefcase, turned off the lights, and headed for home.

He lived half a block off Riverside Drive in one of those grand buildings that was no longer so grand. The paint in the lobby was peeling, and the fake-marble columns in the hallway had cracked and crumbled in places, exposing the plaster underneath the facade. The elevator, an Otis from prewar days, was sufficiently slow to give him time to look through the bills he had collected from the mailbox. When the elevator door finally opened, he found an old woman with too much rouge on her cheeks. She gave a faint whimper of surprise before composing herself and scrunching her face into a hard, untrusting stare. It was the look of a city dweller, tough and forlorn at once, whose children had long ago moved to the suburbs and stopped visiting her. He snorted as she passed on the way to the front door and he ascended to his floor, trying to avoid the thought that someday he would reach the same precipice on which that lady was perched, smudged and shriveled and alone. O Lord, if you exist at all, he prayed, let me not get there. Let this elevator plummet to the basement right now and crush me like a cockroach.

Once inside his apartment the smell of old furniture and plaster comforted him. Everything was in its proper place, that is, the place he had chosen for it when he first moved in. There was the china closet in which he kept his Hummel collection against the far wall, and across from it was the sofa in dark blue upholstery with bear-claw legs like something rescued from a Victorian bestiary. The window curtains, patterned in autumnal oak and maple leaves, showed their age and were strangely reminiscent of the old lady who had stepped out of the elevator. He'd bought the furniture twenty years before, when, elated that he had been granted tenure at the university, he'd gone on a buying spree and loaded his credit cards to the limit. In his apartment he felt truly himself, and he could indulge his secret fantasy of living like an English nobleman. Most days he didn't want to leave, but he was a man of responsibility after all, and teaching was his chosen profession, even if his students were a crew of suburban hooligans with green hair and tattoos on their foreheads.

Saturday, his favorite day, he lay in bed all morning in his silk pajamas under the sheets and rose only to prepare himself a cup of English breakfast tea and buttered toast. He loved his own insouciance. His apartment was a kingdom of this world, to echo a phrase from his favorite Cuban writer. All he was lacking was subjects.

Just then the bell rang. There'd been a robbery on his floor the month before, and so he took the brass-plated poker from the nonfunctional fireplace, stood behind the door at the ready, and looked through the peephole. All he could see was a mop of black hair.

He raised the poker over his head and injecting as much authority as he could into his voice, said, Who is it?

It's me, Ib, Josh Spellman.

Juan Antonio lowered the poker and opened the door. It would have been impolite not to.

Spellman slipped by him and entered the apartment, followed by the stale smell of unwashed denim.

Ib, I understand you write poetry, Spellman said with the careless tone of the recently anointed.

Juan Antonio was taken aback. Fifteen years before, he had written and published a series of sonnets in the symbolist manner under the pseudonym Arturo Prisma. He stopped writing them when, due to the limited rhyming possibilities of English, he fell into free verse, a style he detested as much as the American poets who had popularized it. Juan Antonio was convinced that he was born in the wrong century. He straightened his shoulders and stood in the third position, a habit he had acquired as a young man when he realized that the posture extenuated his already considerable height by a few inches. Even in his slippers he loomed over Spellman. Juan Antonio let his eyes roll down.

That was some years ago, he said. Somewhere in him he felt the spark of flattery growing into a small flame. Stay, please, and have some tea.

I'd prefer coffee, Spellman said.

Good, Juan Antonio said. I have my coffee ground specially for me by a lady in Queens.

Juan Antonio's mood immediately improved. He went into the kitchen and, after a few minutes, returned with a silver tray on which sat an Italian espresso maker, along with two Chinese cups so delicate you could practically see through the porcelain. Next to the cups was a plate with almond and chocolate biscotti, a creamer with heated milk, and two glasses of ice water. His mother had taught him that you must temper the strength of the coffee with the coolness of water.

What distinguishes our coffee, he said, sitting on the sofa next to Spellman, is that we brew it with sugared water. It gives the coffee a silky texture, much different from Italian espresso.

I love Cuban coffee, Spellman said with that peculiar enthusiasm of a liberation theologizer fond of all underdeveloped things. I live on the stuff when I'm in Havana.

Juan Antonio's lips parted into a slow smile.

When were you there? he asked, pouring the coffee carefully so that none of it would dribble outside the cup.

Seven times in the last couple of years, Spellman answered, not without pride.

Juan Antonio grew serious and felt himself stiffening again. He was facing a barbarian of the first rank. What took you there?

My solidarity with the people. To experience the island before it is modernized and turned into an American playground.

Juan Antonio took a deep breath and continued with the preparations. When he was done, he passed a demitasse to Spellman and took the other in his hands. The space between the two men was steeped in the aroma of the best coffee in the world. Juan Antonio waited for Spellman's reaction.

My God, said Spellman, this coffee's incredible!

Have you had coffee like this in Cuba?

No. Not even my girlfriend's mother makes it this good.

Girlfriend? In Cuba?

Yes, Spellman said. He was holding the cup around the sides, ignoring the handle.

Ah, Juan Antonio thought. So that's the solidarity.

She's fifteen, Spellman said. But in Cuba that doesn't mean anything. In Cuba age is relative.

Of course. We Cubans have liberated ourselves from those antiquated notions. He did not allow Spellman to continue. She's probably dark skinned, too, he said. What we call a mulatica, not yet a mulatona.

What's the difference? Spellman asked. Apparently he'd not visited Cuba enough.

About fifteen years and forty pounds. Then you won't be able to handle her. She's a handful as it is, no?

She's vivacious, yes.

And in bed you've never had better. With her mother's blessing and your dollars. Afterward, her mother gives you coffee, which she cuts with ground chickpeas so it'll last longer. Americanos can never tell the difference.

Are you implying that Yareli is a prostitute? A faint blush of anger crossed Spellman's forehead.

Not exactly. She's a survivor. We call them jineteras. We'd do the same thing if we were in her shoes—or her mother's.

Juan Antonio poured a little steamed milk into his coffee to make a cortadito and took his first sip. He closed his eyes and hummed with pleasure. The coffee reminded him of his mother, who died believing that manners and morals are inextricable. In this case, manners had almost made him forget that the young Dr. Spellman had interrupted his morning without so much as a phone call announcing his visit.

And to what do I owe this surprise call, Dr. Spellman? Surely not to let me know that you've read my poetry.

I've just moved into the building, Spellman said. We're neighbors.

Really, Juan Antonio said, barely keeping his horror at bay.

I'm planning an anthology of Cuban poetry in translation, Spellman continued. I thought you might consider contributing a poem to it.

Juan Antonio threw a laugh up to the ceiling. I gave up that silly practice years ago. I have nothing to give you.

Merely saying that relieved him. He did not want to resurrect that part of his life, when he still had hope of being more than a mere academic critic, a backseat driver. He felt a pinprick of nostalgia inside just thinking about those days, when he wrote poetry to his lovers and the world burned with energy. It was the same pinprick he felt when remembering his childhood in Cuba: his mother's hands parting his hair in the morning as she readied him for school, the steaming cup of café con leche the maid prepared for him in the afternoons, the tropical clouds rolling across the cerulean sky of Havana.

Well, I found one published in 1985 in the magazine *The Yellow Egret*. It's called "The Architecture of Princes." Perhaps you recall ...

I do, I do, Juan Antonio said, making a dismissive gesture with his hand. He very much wanted Spellman out of the house now. It's an old piece. I cannot honor your request.

Spellman seemed confused by Juan Antonio's reaction and offered to show him the proposal he'd submitted to the editors. Juan Antonio was steadfast.

Thanks for the coffee, Spellman said. I wish you'd reconsider. The poem is quite good.

Is it really the best coffee you've ever had? Juan Antonio asked as he accompanied the young man to the door.

My taste buds are still jumping, Spellman said walking out.

When he closed the door Juan Antonio realized that he was prouder of his coffee than his poetry. Had he missed his calling? There was a time when his food was celebrated by his guests and he was known as a witty host. Now he had no visitors. His friends had scattered to other parts of the country or preferred to spend their time with children and grandchildren. One by one they dropped away until the last, Ofelia Sánchez de Ortelio, the first lady of Havana society in exile, too, stopped coming, felled by a hiatal hernia that kept her at home dining on dry toast and tea and shriveling up like a yellow prune.

Juan Antonio went to his desk and rifled through his file drawer until he found "The Architecture of Princes." He read it silently first, then a second time aloud, noting its iambic meter, its careful use of end stops, enjambments, and caesuras, and was impressed by how well it was constructed, how resonant of the deepest music of his soul. He spent the rest of the day tinkering with the poem, and by nightfall he had a new draft, solid enough that he was tempted to call Spellman and offer it to him. *Festina lente,* he thought. Hurry slowly. One shouldn't act too rashly in these matters.

When Monday came he reread his revision before his morning class and found the poem awful. He spent the day avoiding Spellman, who rushed from class to class with the energy of a mongoose and, after lunch, held court with eager students on the sidewalks under the faculty offices, where he smoked and laughed with them as if they were his cohorts. Later that week a student came to Juan Antonio extolling Spellman's virtues as a teacher—how passionate he was, how friendly, telling wild stories about his year in Prague. He's brilliant, the student added. Juan Antonio nodded, forced out a smile, and quickly took his leave.

He went home feeling outdated. He'd never been to Prague. London was his city, which he'd visited twice with the reverence due a holy site. He was not interested in any music after Edward Elgar, and the little contemporary rock he had heard sounded like glass cracking under a steamroller. He believed professors professed; they didn't chat, and they didn't share their tobacco with their students. When he entered his apartment and looked in the full-length mirror facing the door, he saw that too many years in the city had given his skin a whitish pallor that his gray suit accentuated. His aquiline nose, which he'd once considered evidence of his aristocratic ancestry, had thickened with age and now drooped over the features of his face like a half-furled jib. His hair had become wispy, like grass sticking out of the snowy dome of his skull, and his eyes had lost the glitter of youthful petulance. More than tired they looked marooned in a sea of irrelevance.

He sat at his desk and looked at the poem again. In the afternoon light it didn't seem so bad; there were moments of grandeur after the volta, and the final couplet, though metrically weak, was a fitting closure to a sonnet Mallarmé might have dreamed of but never written. Mallarmé? To dare think of the French master in connection to this poem was hubris. But why not? There was no one to stop him, only the dim visage of Spellman in his ripped jeans and sneakers, ignoring the past as casually as he ignored the sartorial protocols of the academy.

Unsatisfied with the closing of the poem, Juan Antonio sat at his desk for two hours, refusing to stand until a better one occurred to him. None came, and then, as the afternoon lengthened, he felt the tide of dusk flood the living room until he was an island, utterly alone except for the hum of his Smith Corona electric and the lamp that illuminated the sheet of paper. Along with the shadows came a longing for the past that he was, most days, successful at avoiding. He thought of the ceilings of his childhood house, of the cool tile underfoot where he'd race his toy cars, of the back patio, where he'd play cloak-and-dagger games with imaginary musketeers. He thought of his father scurrying in and out of the house like a shame-ridden mouse, and of his mother, grand and smothering, feeding him cod-liver oil and raw eggs with honey. From her rocking chair she commanded the servants with the authority of a prime minister. He recalled his uncle Pepe, who lived with them because he was mysteriously incapable of work.

On such evenings, Juan Antonio envisioned the geometries of the eternal summer of the tropics, the lines of sun and shade that held all his memories in place, more constant and alive now than they'd ever been. How he longed for the arms of someone who might restore that warmth and that clarity into his crusted heart. His heart, which he'd protected from harm all these years, he now wanted torn, ravaged, plundered. And just as he was drowning in his awful nostalgia, the eyes brimming with tears, the throat choking with grief, the doorbell rang.

It was Spellman come to inquire about the poem. Juan Antonio was grateful and asked him in, insisting he stay for coffee. Spellman said he couldn't stay long. He seemed nervous, and there was a note of desperation in his voice.

Perhaps something stronger. I have some sherry.

Spellman did not reply. Juan Antonio took his silence as assent and brought him the sherry and a plate of chocolates. He poured himself some and raised his glass in a toast.

À votre santé.

Spellman drank his in one gulp, an act Juan Antonio found charming.

I was working on the poem when you rang.

My editors want the manuscript by next week, Spellman said. There seemed to be none of the tensile energy in his voice that Juan Antonio had heard before. He thought he saw Spellman's jaw tremble as he spoke. He poured another glass.

Too much mind, not enough class, Juan Antonio thought. And when the mind failed him, what was poor Spellman left with? Dirty fingernails, a wrinkled shirt.

You'll have the poem by the deadline, he said, sitting in a rocking chair that had belonged to his mother. I'm having trouble with the metrics.

It was fine the way it was, Spellman said, momentarily distracted from whatever ailed him.

To you perhaps.

The young theorist lowered his eyes and grew pensive. Dark cloud.

What? Spellman said.

There's a dark cloud in your eyes and it has nothing to do with the poem. You can confide in me.

Spellman leaned back on the couch and brought his hands to his face.

My girlfriend.

Your Cuban girlfriend?

Yes. When I called last night her mother answered. She said Yareli was engaged to someone else and hung up. I called again several times and the phone was off the hook.

Spellman dropped his hands and let them rest on his thighs. His eyes seemed helpless, as if he were looking out from the bottom of a well from which there is no hope of escape. Juan Antonio had been in the bottom of that well twice in his life and so he felt a closeness to him, but it was not the closeness of compassion. He fought the urge to sit by him and hold him. A brilliant flame flared in his heart and glowed there a moment before disappearing. He reacted to it by forcing Spellman to swallow the truth like a spoonful of cod-liver oil.

She found herself a European, Juan Antonio told him, most probably a Spaniard, middle-aged and approaching retirement.

He promised to bring her and her mother to Spain. There's nothing you can do. Women, especially Cuban women of the present period, are fickle. They'll do anything for a dollar, a euro in this case. Why don't you find yourself someone closer to your background?

Juan Antonio knew that Spellman had no recourse against the scourge of love. He was, after all, a barbarian, without style, and ignorant of the pleasures of dressing in the morning, making his coffee, buying good sherry, and keeping it for occasions such as this in order to counter the devastating effects of paradise lost. Juan Antonio served Spellman another glass.

Better yet, Juan Antonio said, why don't you start taking care of yourself?

What do you mean? Spellman's eyes lost their bovine expression momentarily.

When was the last time you bathed?

I don't know. Two, three days ago.

How can you stand yourself? This mild reproof had the intended effect of awakening Spellman's vanity. Juan Antonio could see it in the way he straightened his neck.

Start by taking a shower. Let the water run over you and breathe in the steam. Buy yourself expensive soap.

Juan Antonio went on, and by the time he was done speaking, he had Spellman dressed in a silk bathrobe, smoking English cigarettes, and smelling like the lord chief baron of the Exchequer. Spellman became ensnared in the web of Juan Antonio's vision. The young theorist squirmed this way and that on the couch trying to free himself.

Tomorrow, Juan Antonio said triumphantly, we'll go to Barney's and you will buy yourself a suit that fits your station in life.

I can't afford Barney's, Spellman said timidly.

But you could afford to keep a hot mulatica in Havana, and her mother, and her whole family, as well? Spellman, Juan Antonio implored in a low whispery register as he leaned over the coffee table. Save yourself!

Under it all, under the gentility of this man of grace and belles lettres, a note of anxiety had sounded, dissonant and flat, and it took all his effort to keep it from coming to the surface and drowning out his advice, his clothes and demitasses, his fine sherry, his porcelain memories of the childhood of privilege he never really had in Cuba.

With a look of terror Spellman stood and rushed out the door, making only a cursory reference to the poem he had come to retrieve. Juan Antonio was at first surprised—he would have used the word dismayed—then he convinced himself that Spellman's sudden exit was evidence that his words had hit the mark. I must be cruel only to be kind, he thought, and started cleaning up, placing the dishes and the two sherry glasses on a painted wooden tray of Russian origin that his last lover had given him. How long ago was that, seven, eight years? He was a twenty-year-old Slav with strong muscles and hands calloused by manual labor, but he was a kitten in bed.

When Juan Antonio reached the kitchen his body began to tremble. The tremor spread from his torso down his arms until he could no longer hold the tray, which went crashing to the floor. He couldn't catch his breath and his chest spasmed with each attempt to draw in air. For a moment he thought the end had come. Slowly his long body slid down the door frame to the floor, where it came to rest surrounded by shards of porcelain, sharp jags of crystal, and pieces of dark Belgian chocolate. Then the weeping came, profound and unfathomable, like a flood of black water. He was twelve years old. He was lost in a room without walls. He cried a long time, and when he had no more tears in him, he noticed a finger smudge on the refrigerator door that he had missed on his last cleaning. He stared at the smudge, thinking he needed to wipe it off but making no effort to stand.

He was too old for this, too old to fall apart over a young fool who had not yet found the limits of his talent, too old for melodrama. There was no such thing as saving yourself. There was only the awareness of the moment of your decrepitude. Your head is an empty gourd, a teacher once told him. Fill it. Juan Antonio tried, with every bit of knowledge he could find. He could feel the emptiness, not just in his head, where all that knowledge had turned to smoke, but in his heart, croaking with need. He could hear the wind rushing through the conduits of his blood. He could hear the bellow of a distant bull, a lone cricket chirping, a dove cooing at the edges of a field smoldering with wasted love. Finally he stood and went to the window as the city lights came on and people in their heavy coats rushed home, indifferent to human sorrow but carrying it within themselves like a seed that would sprout in the most unlikely moment, just when they thought they were beyond it, when they thought they had saved themselves. No help for the young barbarian, no help for the old belletrist. His gourd was rattling with the broken husks of beautiful letters.

STORYTELLER

She did it out of shame, she did it out of rage, vertigo, romance, ambition, disdain, indifference, selfishness, self-loathing—torch singer, hah—wanting to erase her mistake and get the little monster of her lust flushed out with plumbing fluid. Why didn't she get an abortion from a proper doctor or leave me at the front door of an orphanage, wrapped in swaddling clothes? Because she wanted to live a bolero. I found her old diary under her bed after she died, and from it I learned Papa was not my father. She did it because not doing it meant raising the child as if it were her husband's. In the end that's what happened. My real father was a handyman, a young buck from the country, just this side of manhood, with those country eyes that could be sad or wise or stupid or impenetrable and that he didn't know how to avert.

But it could have been anyone: the gardener, the grocer, the itinerant barber who worked the neighborhood. She snared the handyman and he was too afraid or humble or hungry to say, No, Madam. Thank you, but no. If I do this there's no telling where it will lead.

She led him to her bed, where she spread herself out for him, ample and open. She had her way with him. I feel no urge to find him. I am content making him up: Gomercindo, Fajardo, Longino—she didn't write the name. Curly black hair, skin cured by the sun, smooth hairless chest, wiry, veiny arms, and hands cracked from day labor, smelling of hard earth, soft water, and the breeze sifting through sugar cane.

Nothing to do with love. She shoved the boy away when she was done, told him to go back to his miserable town and never contact her again. The boy's seed took and sprouted. What to do? Lock her shame in pleasure? Go with the boy, find him, let him do with her what he wanted. It was a bolero without escape. The bottle of liquid lye in the garage: for lead pipes, for sewers. She poured it into herself, bathed me in the stuff, let it burn like hell potion. For three days her womb sizzled and sputtered, sending forth red foam and stench. Her husband wept and screamed and pleaded to call the doctor. No, shaking her head. He'd bring a santera, a babalawo, anyone. No, sweat like beads of sin on her forehead, her insides melting. No. On the fourth day there was no pain, just a cold fluid in her veins that made her shiver and go into spasms, her body stiff like wood, her tongue rolling out of her mouth. Then indifference, then a kick inside and another, the creature still in her alive, knocking.

¡Pinga! she yelled. ¡Coño! And then she passed out, seeming dead to the husband, who rushed out and got the first doctor he could find, a veterinarian who lived down the block.

Lye, the vet said. She's got lye in her system but the fetus is alive. Fetus he called me. I was. That's what I heard in my mother's pages. Animals don't do this, he said, making a scientific observation, which he meant literally but the husband interpreted to mean his wife was lower than an animal and threw a punch at him, missing the vet's jaw and landing squarely on the wall. He screamed and doubled over holding his right hand.

Or that, the vet said. Ever the man of science, he checked the husband's hand for broken bones, and finding none, he wrapped it in gauze, for the placebo effect, and left the house.

Blindness is a labyrinth. Once you're in you can't leave. You walk. You stand. Everywhere is the center. On the other side of the room, across the river and into the trees.

Mama inserted the plastic bottle into herself and squeezed. I lived. Bleared, blind, born. Went from one labyrinth with walls to another without, birth my sin. She was at the center, waiting for me. She sang boleros only I heard, in the hallways of the new labyrinth. I tried to find a way out, my hands stretched out into the gray fog, reaching for a door. I told stories. Every sentence leading farther in, every word bifurcating, in the center the monster, pawing the bed, spewing fire out of her cunt. She had sex with a young hot bull, she had sex with an ass, she had sex with a toad, a fish, a worm, a beaky bird. She tried to kill me before I was born. She looked back. How do you leave the only thing you've known? She bore me. I bore her. We were each other's sin, each other's hatred. When she died, she clucked like a sorry hen, then fluttered. When she died I didn't shed a tear. Not in me, not out of me. I entered another labyrinth, an acid wind cutting through. Lye. Havana was a labyrinth. Cubop City was a labyrinth where all doors lead in or out. I heard the roar of her breathing, the pounding of her heart. No walls. Deeper in I go.

MELODRAMA

You are in love. You seek (and find) your lover in all that surrounds you—the pens and pencils that blossom like spiny flowers from the cup on your desk; the faint buzz of the printer in harmony with the hum of the city; that sheet on which your mother embroidered fantails once. If you eat a strawberry, it is the lover's lips you are biting; if you inadvertently brush against a bare arm on the subway it is your lover's skin you feel. At dusk it is the lover's voice you hear coming from the radio and her smell, attar of musk and moss, that wakes you at midnight. Her breath is your breath, her moans your moans. All love is erasure, the bicycle you ride to her neighborhood. Then you realize she's not there but on the other side of town. Every mirror gives you back a shadow.

It is not a dream. Beyond the window of your study is a field overlooking the sea; you watch yellow flowers bend with the wind. You'd like to be on one of those sailboats that come and go with amazing grace. From the small cottage on the hill she comes down to you. She wears a stern look like an executioner puts on when coming to meet his victim. You are sitting on the grass with your knees drawn to your chest, the sun warming your body, your mind liberated—momentarily—from duty and ambition. She stands over you and blocks the sun and suddenly a shiver runs through you. You ask her to sit and she refuses, comes straight to the truth. She no longer loves you and is leaving, going home. No, no, you say, we'll work it out. After your entreaties fail, your strategy changes to feigned anger. You stand, loom over her, and cry out, calling her thankless and duplicitous, a liar, a witch, but the anger is shallow, lacking self-preservation to give it solidity, and soon it turns to weeping. Why? you ask, and the question becomes a demand. Anger again, then the tear floods and sigh tempests. Ah, melodrama!

You go inside the house, walk out, then go inside again. What to do? To do what? Standing at the door to the bedroom, you watch her pack all her white dresses, her blue jeans, her work boots, books, CDs. But how will she get them to the road? You will not give her your car, you will not lend her your wheelbarrow or the donkey cart or the burlap sacks in which once you carried coconuts. All the time she's been avoiding your sight, and when she finally looks at you, her eyes have no fire in them, only disdain. You try a rational approach. That, too, is flimsy, without the pillars of indifference to secure it:

125

You ask in a kind and measured tone for an explanation. She is almost finished packing and is rifling through the drawers in search of a last article to put into the suitcase. This is her story and she knows it. There is a splotch of red on her neck where yesterday a bee stung her. What kind of bee is it that would change her so irrevocably? Love is a balloon, she says without speaking. At first it is full to bursting with warm air. As the air cools it escapes. In time the balloon deflates and falls to the ground, a despicable flat piece of red latex. But your toes, you cry, your lips, the slope of your belly, and you smoke an imaginary cigarette, have an imaginary drink in a poorly lit bar in an outer borough of Cubop City, where nothing ever happens and one bolero follows the next forever through dusk. Later that night you sit at the edge of the bed and wonder how you will tolerate the emptiness that has taken residence inside the house and sits on your chair speaking a language in reverse. Amardolem, ha!

MR. HANDLEBAR

The man with the handlebar mustache appears at the door holding a dead fish, a large brown grouper with bulging milky eyes. He tells Angel the fish is good and fresh, and with that he enters the apartment and sets the fish down on the table. Flap! There is no Amanda this time. Angel takes the grouper to the kitchen and cleans it. Holding the curved scaling knife in his hand, he thinks that if there was a time to get back at his attacker, it is now. If only he lived in the Midwest, Mr. Handlebar would not come to him with a grouper. Angel would not be cleaning it and he'd not be tempted to strike Handlebar with the scaling knife. If this were the Midwest, he'd have brought corn or apples. He wouldn't have known about groupers, let alone how to catch one.

The man with the handlebar mustache goes to the refrigerator, takes a beer, and sits at the table. He is eager to befriend Angel and asks about his woman. There is no woman, Angel says. A fulsome necromancer, Handlebar insists. Angel tries to smile but his lips don't spread, his teeth don't show.

What Angel doesn't say to this man is that he broke up with Amanda just over a year ago. It was nothing in particular. There was arguing and recrimination and broken promises and betrayals. She claimed he was a political brute. He called her a red menace and an antipapist. Just to irk her he went to church, told her it was comforting. She yelled that that was a deal breaker, whatever that meant. You talk to the dead, he tried arguing back. I don't go around molesting children. Huh? he said. Priests, she said, you know, then locked herself in the bathroom. Some nights it was him watching television or her communicating with her spirits. Then things grew quiet between them. It was the quiet of desolation. The desolation became indifference and the indifference led to Amanda one day walking out. Among her last words to him were, The man with the handlebar mustache will come back into your life. Angel didn't pay attention. He was a wreck on the shoals of self-pity.

There he is, drinking Angel's beer. For a moment he wishes Amanda were back. She would know what to do. He cleans the fish and rubs the outside with mojo until the kitchen is redolent of garlic and lime. He hears Handlebar at the table smacking his lips after each sip of beer. Angel wills away his discomfort and dresses the grouper, stuffs sprigs of rosemary into the gills, covers it with aluminum foil, and puts it in the

oven at 325° F. Then he opens a beer and sits across from
Handlebar, who is, as is the habit with men of his ilk, twirling his mustache. He smiles, but the hair on his upper lip is so
thick that only his two front teeth show, a large, happy rodent.

Did you try to kill me? Angel asks in a confrontational
tone. My former lover, the necromancer and soothsayer in
training, claims you did. Did you?

Handlebar does not change his expression. Instead of
answering he takes a sip of his beer, then brings his tongue
up and around to lick the foam off his mustache. In the blink
of an eye he's gone from rodent to feline. Long straight hairs
grow from his muzzle and his eyes are yellow.

Did you, Angel asks, knife someone at the corner of Twen-
tieth and Seventh?

Handlebar blinks slowly. He is still smiling.

Angel stares at him for a long time. Handlebar stares back,
blinking those slow alligator blinks of his. Now he is a reptile
with a long green snout and mouth lined with teeth. He could
bite off Angel's head. Angel is growing concerned about the
fish in the oven—what use is a burned grouper?—but he's
determined to get an answer. Finally Handlebar speaks.

I am your hometown butcher.

What are you saying? I have no hometown.

Everyone does. Remember? La Habana, Sabana, Banana.
I had sides of beef hanging on the shop windows and calf
heads under them. Your mother would come in for boliche
or palomilla or picadillo. I was an artist and meat was my
medium. My shop smelled of blood and sinew. Better than
a rose patch.

Angel doesn't remember going to a butcher shop with his mother. How does Handlebar know he's from Havana? If he is a butcher, why has he brought along a fish? And why doesn't he speak with an accent?

Would you like another beer? Angel asks. It's a chess game he's playing and Handlebar's a master.

Yes, Handlebar says without hesitation.

Angel gets two beers, checks on the fish, and by the time he returns to the table, Handlebar has turned into an amoeba, transparent and damp, with the handlebar mustache floating in the cytoplasm.

My ancestors came from passive blubbery, he says. And you, my child, he adds like a priestly protozoan, what is your story?

I want to know if you tried to kill me.

I am a master with the knife, says Handlebar. If I'd wanted to kill you, I would know precisely where to strike.

But you are here, Angel says, sounding shrill.

Because I am not there.

Who did it then? Why did you come to my home?

Handlebar raises his wet, goopy hands and shrugs his shoulders.

Amanda sent me. She gave me the fish, he says, slurping the beer.

Angel can see the liquid dissolve into the cytoplasm. He has nothing to say. There's a wall between him and everything he thought had been real. Nothing in his life has connection to anything else. His life is an Aristotelian failure. Then he smells the fish cooking. At least there is that. Fish appears, is cleaned and dressed, put into the oven, watched over, and after an hour, fish is ready. Progression. Forward movement in time and all the events sequenced. Life should be a recipe. He opens the oven and pulls out the grouper. It is magnificent, golden and crisp on the outside, and when he cuts into it, it lets off a cloud of steam, a sure sign that it has remained moist on the inside. He can smell the ocean coming out of the pan and the earth, too.

When he goes back to the living room, he sees a moist trail leading to the door. Handlebar has left, without saying good-bye, without even finishing his beer. Angel returns to the kitchen, serves himself a large chunk of the grouper, and spoons pan drippings over it, topping everything with several slices of tomato and onion. He opens a bottle of white wine he's kept in the refrigerator and sits at the table. Momentarily he forgets about Handlebar and Amanda and the knifing. He begins slowly, tasting every bite. Then, suddenly, he tears large chunks of the flesh with his hands and stuffs them into his mouth. He eats like a barbarian. He eats like tomorrow never comes. It doesn't.

WAR OF
THE WORLDS

Somehow Angel managed to get it all: the three-bedroom house with flower beds in the back, the sweet wife all smiles and tenderness, two teenage daughters, sunlight gleaming off their auburn hair and eager eyes. They lived in a suburban development at the edge of a forest. Beyond the backyard were tall oaks and pines, a shadowy place where deer sometimes gathered and where he occasionally saw an angry-looking stray dog come out of the shadows to nose around the grass and piss on the flowers. He'd go back there to get away from the family and smoke cigarettes. He came from the heat and sun of the tropics, and he never felt comfortable in the forest, but it was his only escape other than work. The ground was damp and musty and the canopy pressed down on him. Large wolf spiders looked lethal and purple beetles stuck to the underside of leaves, dropping on his shirt as he walked under them. Once he spied an insect that had huge pincers in the back. It rested on a fallen log, and when he poked it with a stick, the thing flew straight at his face. That's what you get for going into the forest primeval, he said to himself afterward, drinking a whiskey to calm his nerves.

A few days later as he smoked his cigarettes a safe distance from the woods, he noticed a group of airplanes over the trees. They were propeller types, B-17s and B-24s, flying in battle formation. He called his daughters outside and said, Look, girls, they're going to war. They ran around the yard yelling, War, war, and his wife, hearing the commotion, came outside and said, What war? He shrugged and smoked more cigarettes.

This happened over the next few days. At first, whenever they heard the noise of the engines, they rushed outside and marveled that there could be so many planes on this earth. They pointed to their insignia. They waved at them. One of the girls thought she saw a pilot waving back. He has a mustache, she said, and a white bandana flapping in the wind. Angel thought of Errol Flynn and smiled. It was war. His wife bought a big American flag and unfurled it whenever the planes passed over, claiming the boys needed all the support they could get. They flew in V-formation during the day and at night, and the family cheered loudly. Go get 'em, boys. Give 'em hell!

After two weeks they couldn't sleep because the engine roar made their sternums rattle; they couldn't have dinner without the windows trembling and his wife's ceramic figurines dancing dangerously close to the edge of the mantel. Three fell to the floor and shattered, including a Lladró shepherd girl that had belonged to her Spanish grandmother.

Angel developed ticks—a continual blinking and involuntary movements of his limbs that kept him from concentrating. From frustration he yelled at his wife, who yelled at his daughters, who yelled at him, the circle broken only during those few hours when the planes weren't flying. The situation became intolerable. He started spending more time away from home. He sat in his car every night after work, the windows rolled up, the radio off, listening to nothing but the traffic on the interstate whooshing by. He joined some of his coworkers at a local bar where drinks were cheap and didn't come home until midnight when he knew his wife would be asleep from the effects of booze and sleeping pills.

Where were those planes going? What retro war had begun and was spreading its poison into his family life? Every morning he woke to his haggard wife, his harping daughters, and that stray dog that came out of the woods. He thought of buying a gun and shooting it. Boom, right between the eyes. Work suddenly became a solace, the bar a sought-after refuge where he could converse about those things he cared about—sports, women, movies—never the war, since none of his friends brought it up. Come to think of it, it seemed as if only his family was afflicted, only his house that had vintage planes flying over it and dread filling up its rooms like thick, impassable mucilage.

It was at the bar that he met Nancy with the size 11 feet. She wore her blonde hair short and had a long neck exacerbated by a small round face. His friends were arguing about

NASCAR racing when he noticed her sitting next to him eating a hot dog. There was a spot of mustard on her cheek. Finally, he took a bar napkin, said, Excuse me, and wiped it off. Instead of telling him off as he expected, she turned red, like paprika, like a bullfighter's muleta flashing in the bull-ring. She patted both cheeks nervously, then asked if it was all gone. Yes, he said. Don't worry. Mustard is like cream cheese. It gets on everything. He bought her a cosmopolitan. They talked about nothing in particular and that was that. She was there the next night, sitting on the other side of the U-shaped bar eating a burger, no mustard this time. He took his drink and moved next to her and said something stupid like, I like the view better from here. He bought her two cosmopolitans and he had two martinis, dry, straight up with olives, enough drink to loosen them up. She told him about her lousy job at a nonprofit organization. Nonprofits don't make money, that's their problem, she said. I'm looking for a career change. He tried not to be sardonic and described his job at the factory assembling scuba oxygen valves.

It's a big responsibility, he said. Someone could drown or die from nitrogen narcosis if the valve isn't calibrated just right. It's a terrible death; your blood vessels fill with gas and your blood boils. High stress, he emphasized, fishing in his glass for an olive. But after ten years it's second nature. It sounded like he was boasting but he wasn't. The truth was that the job kept him out of the house for eight hours a day. He didn't mention the war, though he was tempted. He could've talked to Nancy about anything that night. Instead they discussed politics, and for some reason they got into mercury pollution. He'd ordered fish and chips. Before he knew it, it was midnight. He asked if she was going to be there the following night. She said she was going on a trip.

Next week, she said. I'll be here next week.

She was back the next week but she had changed. She wore new makeup that made her look vampish and a different hairdo, which fell asymmetrically down the left side of her head, and she was wearing a pink turtleneck that disguised her llama neck. From five thirty to eight o'clock they talked. They talked a tide of language, a storm of words. By eight thirty he'd had four drinks, enough to say, I'm attracted to you. She looked at him, eyes flattened by alcohol, and suggested they go to her place. I'll cook something up, she said.

They wound up in bed, had sex like vultures, and forgot about dinner. When he was done he turned over and saw outlined by the light coming through the window two white mounds rising from the end of the bed. He looked under the sheets and beheld the biggest feet he'd ever seen on a woman, the Popocatepetl and Ixtaccihuatl of feet. They were so large they could only be seen in sections—the heel, the arch, the instep, the toes. He became so excited he slithered onto her again. He roared, he bellowed, he wailed, he whinnied, he honked and chirped and hooted and clonked. Nancy was a turbulent ocean beneath him, a hurricane above him, but it was her feet that captivated him, not the dirty words she whispered in his ear or the rhythmic gyrations of her pelvis. He had found it at last, the place beyond heaven, the protoparadise, and it was her feet that led him there.

They stopped the pretense of meeting at the bar and went to her apartment every night after work, where they made the bed shake and the walls vibrate and the ceiling lift off the crossbeams. He went home punctually at midnight. He wanted his wife to think he was still spending his time at the bar with his friends, but it was too late for that. The war had gotten worse. More planes, more noise. He could hear the whine of Spitfires, P-51s, and Messerschmitts dogfighting over the house, their engines strained to the limit as they swooped and looped over and around one another, machine guns blazing and the *ack-ack* of antiaircraft fire making fiery blossoms in midair. Where did it all come from? In the living room was his wife sitting on the sofa, silent, murderous. Not even the sleeping pills were working. Her eyes were ablaze with hatred and exhaustion, her skin aglow with outrage. I know what you're up to, she said. Who's the slut? Then she went off to the guest room and locked the door behind her. The girls were already asleep, or in what passed for sleep in their house, and he was glad not to witness their twitching faces, their bloodshot eyes. He went straight to bed and left the house in the morning before anyone else was up. It was easier that way.

The following night as he pulled into the driveway he noticed that a suburban quiet had returned to the house. He looked up into the night sky and all he could see was stars, millions of them, dotting the darkness. He got out of the car and rushed into the house. All the furniture was gone. Even the curtains had been pulled from their runners, leaving the rods dangling obliquely across the windows.

Upstairs there was only the king-size bed they'd bought the previous year and his dresser. On it was a note that read simply, I surrender. You win. Win what? he asked himself, this gravelike silence, this emptiness? He moved from room to room, gradually sinking deeper into the quicksand of melancholia. In his daughters' room he finally leaned his back against the wall and looked to the ceiling, wanting to cry so that the sadness of the world would evaporate. He couldn't. The sadness grew dense inside him. He thought of the stray, that hound stalking his backyard. He thought of his girls being raised by a strange man in a checkered shirt and suspenders, an electrical engineer like his wife's father, making much more money than Angel ever would. For a moment he felt nostalgic about the war and wished for the planes to return. I'll get rid of that dog, I promise, he imagined telling his wife. It was madness.

He left the empty house and returned to Nancy's apartment. He knocked a number of times before she answered. She stood before him in a bathrobe, her hair disheveled, her neck rising out of her torso like a jet of flesh and bone on top of which floated her small round head like a doll's. Behind her the figure of a man flashed from the bedroom to the bathroom and shut the door. He pushed her aside and rushed into the apartment, ready to rip the guy apart with his bare hands and choke that long neck of hers until she turned blue in the face. A part of him remained cool, however, and that part prevailed. He thought, Why should I kill this woman for whom I have no wish to be with beyond an hour or two, dimmed by alcohol, driven only by a voyeur's desire to behold her feet?

Nancy's postcoital conversation was limited to the non-profit sector. God, she was dull. And now she had someone else in the house. His rage was gone and he felt pity for the man and pitied himself as well. Nancy yelled that she was going to call the cops if he didn't leave immediately. She picked up a vase from her bookcase and made as if she was going to throw it at him. He looked down at her feet, long and narrow as Roman triremes on the wine-dark sea of the rug, and found them ridiculous. That was okay. To the victor belong the spoils, he said to himself. He turned on his heels and went downstairs to the parking lot. The war had begun again. Only this time it was on the ground. Soldiers with bayonets fixed to their rifles ran between the cars in the parking lot, and the flash and roar of artillery approached ineluctably in Angel's direction.

RAINING
BASEBALLS

Just as you fix your sight on a ball leaving your father's bat, another reaches the apogee of its arc and begins to descend a few feet away. You run to that, hoping you'll have enough time to catch it and come back to get the other. Then a whack sounds and there is a third and almost immediately a fourth coming out of the sun, then several more in quick succession, followed by an old typewriter, a twirling pig, three flapping chickens, a statuette of the Virgin Mary and a flügelhorn, a coffeepot, dozens of books, a machete glinting in the sunlight, an automobile tire, a tricycle, a wife, many lovers, one infant enjoying the ride, a grandmother playing solitaire, another grandmother stuffing sausages, thousands of pages darkened by a language that isn't yours, a black panther, a school of yellow fish, a telescope for looking out, a microscope for looking in, fishhooks and harpoons and Captain Ahab and Emma Bovary and Maritornes the wench, no Don Quixote but a Humbert Humbert, an Úrsula Iguarán, a Père Goriot, a duck, an inkwell, a feast of cannibals, a pot of beans, angels and demons fighting for your soul, a boy building sand castles in the make-believe beach of his wanting, where an island boomerangs around his head.

When it is all done, the field is steaming from all the objects, the names, the melting memories. You wind your way to where your father was standing. Now only the bat is left next to home plate. You feel defrauded. Who could ever catch so much in a lifetime, let alone fifteen minutes? You pick up the bat and go in search of him. He has his back to you, urinating in some bushes behind the dugout. He turns, but he is not your father. His face the indeterminate face of Don Nadie, a nobody. You ask him the meaning of this. You were simply fun-going at first, catching balls he batted out to you, and suddenly the world rained down. His answer comes slowly, as if he were searching for the right words. You wanted to play, he says. Baseball, you say, not life. What's the difference? he asks. Where's my father? you ask. You have no father, there never was any father. You made him up in order to play the game. How about my mother? She's out in the field, in triplicate.

You ask him who he is and all you get in response is a half smile. He walks out of the bushes and into a car that vanishes down the road. Now you look over the mess on the field and wonder if you should clean it up. You decide that while it may be your life, it is not your responsibility. You step down into the dugout and put the glove into the bag. Somehow you missed your mother coming at you. You look back at the field one last time and there she is, as the man said, in bed retching with pain, in the hospital gurney surrounded by curtains, in the hot night soaping herself in her bath.

BENNIE ROJAS AND THE ROUGHRIDERS

The morning Bennie Rojas boarded the plane for Las Vegas, Cuba was already beginning to fade, and all his troubles were but flickering specks in a distant predawn sky. In the seat to Benny's right was one of the cooks from Tropicana, the grandest nightclub in the world, where Benny himself worked as a twenty-one dealer. To the left was a taciturn man with a scar that ran from his ear to his chin. He'd gotten on in Miami, where the plane stopped on its way west, and said nothing for five and a half hours. Naturally, Bennie assumed he did not speak any Spanish. Tough guys, Bennie thought. There's nothing you can do about them. And so he spent the whole trip talking to the cook, a fellow with a pencil-thin mustache and a head shaped like an eggplant.

Orlando Leyva was from the city of Matanzas, which he insisted on calling the Athens of Cuba.

There are more poets in Matanzas than in the rest of the island combined, he said. They are like songbirds, and on Sunday you can hear them in the park reciting their verses at the pretty women passing by. Many of them commit suicide because they are unhappy in love. Many others are homosexuals in disguise.

Bennie asked him if that was also part of the glory of Matanzas.

No, hombre. But it is the truth. The city has that name because the Spaniards killed a lot of Indians there. It is also called the Venice of Cuba because there are seventeen bridges crossing over three rivers. Havana has nothing like that. Havana is too big and dirty. It's a piece of shit.

Bennie wanted to ask him why he had gone to Havana in the first place, why he didn't stay in Athens listening to all the songbirds, but just then the plane began bucking.

Orlando clutched the armrest and began sweating. Rivulets ran down his face and moistened his collar.

Ay, Dios, he said. We're going to fall.

Bennie tried to comfort Orlando by patting his hand. The man with the scar was like a sphinx. After a few minutes the turbulence subsided. Orlando stopped sweating and settled back into his seat.

The only reason I'm going to Las Vegas is that they promised me a job, he said.

They promised me a job, too, Bennie said. I'm told Lansky is a man of his word.

Unless he isn't.

Unless he isn't, Bennie repeated. If it weren't for politics, Havana would be paradise, he added. Maybe Las Vegas is paradise.

Las Vegas is in the desert.

Where do you think the Garden of Eden was located, chico, in the Caribbean?

Waiting for his bags in the claim area, Bennie concluded that Las Vegas was not paradise, but it was better than being unemployed in Havana with a wife who was always barking at him. He met her after his previous fiancée broke off their engagement and ran off with a man who owned three hardware stores and a house in Miramar. María Cristina was the first woman who showed any interest in him after the breakup and so he married her. In one month he realized he had made the biggest mistake of his life. First, María Cristina complained about the heat, as if it were Bennie's fault. Why don't you buy me an air conditioner? All the neighbors have them. Bennie thought that was a good idea and got an air conditioner from one of the neighbors who was leaving the country. Next María Cristina complained that her clothes were out of style. Bennie took her to El Encanto, the most luxurious department store in Havana, and bought her expensive dresses imported from New York and Paris. Then she asked for a late-model car. Bennie took out a loan and acquired a 1955 Oldsmobile owned briefly by a corrupt politician. It was a beautiful red and white machine that turned all the neighbors' heads. When María Cristina saw it, she refused to get in it, saying she didn't like the color scheme. Soon Bennie was staying up nights worrying about how to please her without going bankrupt.

It occurred to him that he should skim some chips or pass cards or take a hit. Only once in his ten-year career had Bennie cheated a customer, a German businessman who was up thirty thousand dollars on the house. The floor manager gave him a certain look and Bennie used his considerable dexterity with the cards to take back the money, plus an additional twenty thousand dollars in a note. His bosses gave him a gold watch for his performance, but for Bennie the watch was a symbol of his dishonesty, and so he sold it to a friend for five hundred dollars. He still remembered the poor German's face as it went from ruddy ebullience to pallid defeat in two hours. Other than that, Bennie was an honest man, given to simple pleasures. After work he had a Cuba libre with the other dealers and went home to his wife, such as she was.

No one had anything on him, except that the revolutionaries who had driven Batista out considered all casino employees to be worms feeding on the dung heap of capitalism, as Fidel himself had said. Individual ethics counted for nothing. It was only a matter of time before the revolutionaries came after Bennie and put him in one of their decrepit jails.

After Fidel took over, the casinos remained open for some time. Tourists were still coming to Cuba, suckers willing to have their money taken while they drank themselves silly on daiquiris. Bennie would see an Americano at the table with a couple of gorgeous Cuban redheads wrapped around him and say to himself, Man, if only I had the money, I'd be right there next to him. Then one day two men came around asking if anyone wanted to go work in Las Vegas.

Las Vegas? Where is that? Bennie asked. In the middle of nowhere, one of the men said. But soon it's going to be the next Havana. You schmucks want to stay here and rot? *Schmuck* was a word Bennie had never heard. The man talking kept straightening his tie as he spoke. He looked like a twenty-year-old version of John Garfield except that he spoke in a gravelly falsetto.

I have a wife, Bennie started to say. Then he remembered his crazy wife. This was the perfect opportunity to escape his lousy marriage and all that he feared was coming to the island. When he told María Cristina that night about the job offer, she yelled, I'm not going to Las Vegas or anywhere else! You don't have to, he said meekly. As soon as she heard he'd be making three times his Tropicana salary, her mood changed. She became excited and started making plans for all the money he'd be sending home. Bennie nodded. He said not to worry. He'd be home in a year. For a brief moment she looked at him. Then tears welled in her eyes and she threw her arms around him.

Two weeks later Bennie was at Las Vegas Airport, waiting for his bags with Orlando and three of his culinary colleagues. The man with the scar led the five of them to a Ford station wagon and drove them to a motel off Ranch Drive. It was mid-July and the heat rose visibly from the asphalt. Bennie complained, but the cooks, used to the infernal atmosphere of commercial kitchens, went on with their chatter. Paradise indeed. Another man met them at the motel and gave each of them a room key. Bennie's was number 207.

Good number to play, he said to Orlando. Number two is butterfly. Number seven is seashell.

Mine is one twelve. One is horse. Twelve is whore, Orlando said. Not too good. That Chinese system is foolishness. There are better ways to make money.

Then the man announced that someone would be by the next morning at seven thirty and left.

For seven years Bennie lived in that motel, caught between a dead-end present and a useless nostalgia for a truncated past. His one friend, Orlando, spoke only of the perfect demi-glace he'd concocted that morning or the bread he'd baked for lunch or the celebrity who'd entered the kitchen and offered his compliments on the salmon mousse. When Bennie tried to inspire him with more expansive topics, such as baseball or women, a distant look came over Orlando's face and he switched the conversation back to kitchen matters. Bennie worked the graveyard shift because nights were hardest for him to spend alone. He'd sleep mornings as much as he could, until noon or so. He'd shower, pick up the local paper, and go to a cafeteria on Sahara, where he'd have two eggs fried over-easy, bacon, toast, and bad American coffee. The rest of the time was his to do as he wanted. He napped, read the paper again, and, in the cool months, walked streets that led nowhere but back into themselves. He began at 11 PM but often worked a double, starting at three o'clock and going straight through until seven the next morning. The summer was too hot to do anything but sit in air-conditioning; the winter was high season, and Joey, his pit boss, threw as much work at him as he could handle. María

Cristina, who had since moved to Miami, sent him divorce papers, which he signed and sent back.

Las Vegas would never be another Havana. There was no ocean to look at, only desert and fancy casinos where the tourists dropped their money. Mostly there was a lot of dust, which got in his eyes and made him teary, as if he wasn't teary enough already. There were plenty of women, beautiful ones, but none was accessible to him, a simple dealer from the tropics with a thick Cuban accent—like Desi Arnaz chewing on a raw steak, Joey once said—and the looks of a Galician grocer. The way to attract women, an uncle of his told him long ago, was to impress them with your power and your wealth. You don't give them money, the uncle had advised. You shower them with it. The woman needs to see you as a god, and those attributes are the closest we humans have to divinity. Just when Bennie had resigned himself to a life of celibacy, he met a woman, a round Mexican who cooked him fiery dishes and made sex like a Zapotec beast. She always brought enough food—enchiladas, tacos, moles—for him and Orlando, who lived downstairs. Her name was Mercedes. She took care of both of them, but she had her eye on Bennie. *Barriga llena, corazón contento,* she would say with a sparkle in her eye, expecting any moment that he would say back to her the magic words.

As he sat outside his room on his day off, Bennie heard a commotion on the first level of the motel, followed by a woman's voice that sounded very much like Mercedes screaming, ¡puto, cabrón, hijo de la chingada! He rushed down the steps and saw Orlando the cook on the floor, leaning against the brick wall outside his room with a butcher knife stuck halfway into his chest. His eyes were glazed and bloody saliva hung from his lips. Orlando babbled something about someone taking twenty thousand. He looked up at Bennie before letting out a long sigh like a train coming to its final stop, and then his head drooped softly to the side.

Bennie's first instinct was to go back inside and pretend he'd seen nothing. Instead, he looked around to make sure no one else had witnessed the killing, maneuvered Orlando away from the wall with great difficulty, and dragged him back into the room. Bennie shut the door and turned the air-conditioning as high as it would go, figuring it would help preserve Orlando. He sat on the unmade bed and tried to light a cigarette. His hands were shaking, so it took four tries before he could bring the match to the tip and take the first drag. Sure, he'd seen plenty of people die, like his mother and her sisters, and a cousin who died of leukemia, but never like this, with a knife sticking out of them and their last words about money. This would never happen in Cuba, he thought, then thought again. Of course it would. Still, at the moment he wanted to be back there in his old apartment on Virtudes Street, where his parents had lived and their parents before them, now occupied by his revolution-crazed cousin, Leida.

Bennie surveyed the room and spied a half-full bottle of DonQ rum on the dresser, which he could reach without having to stand up. Two healthy swigs and he considered the situation. Calling the police wasn't an option. They'd snoop, and his bosses weren't fond of snooping. So he called Joey, his pit boss, at the casino—he'd know what to do—and waited for him.

When Joey showed up at the motel three hours later and saw the cook lying on the carpet, his first words were *holy fucking shit*. Orlando's face had turned gray and rigor mortis was setting in, no matter that it was damned cold in the room. Those were Joey's second words: It's damn cold in here, followed by, What were you fighting about?

Fight? Bennie kept to himself the fact that he heard Mercedes screaming just before he found the cook. Joey, he said, I didn't kill Orlando. He was my friend.

Friends kill each other all the time. Why didn't you take the knife out of him? The longer he's dead the harder it's going to be. And next time you put a shower curtain under him. That way blood doesn't go on the rug.

You do it, Joey. You take the knife out. I couldn't even watch my mother kill a chicken.

Didn't they teach you anything in that damn country of yours? Fucking Latin lover can't get his hands dirty.

Joey looked long and hard at Bennie; then he kneeled next to Orlando and jiggled the knife handle. Blood's pretty much set. We won't be needing the curtain. Before he'd finished saying the word *curtain,* he had the knife out and was holding it next to his head. It was a huge, nasty thing. For an instant, Bennie had the image of the blade entering Orlando and causing massive damage to his inner organs. The thought made him swoon.

This is a job for the roughriders, Joey said and made a call from the hotel phone. In thirty minutes two men showed up.

One was tall and slim and wore a gray suit. The other, short and heavyset, was wearing a purple shirt and beige pants. Bennie noticed that the short man had a tomato-sauce stain on his right pant leg. The men looked at dead Orlando on the floor and proceeded to ransack drawers, pulling them out of the dresser and upending their contents on the body. When they were done with the drawers, they took the bed apart, then started on the closets and rifled through Orlando's clothes, discarding them in every direction. Finally one of them turned to Bennie, who was now standing in a corner of the room and said, Where's the money?

Money? Bennie asked innocently.

Now the three men were looking at him waiting for an answer.

I don't know about no money. Bennie's legs were shaking and his throat was beginning to tighten as it did every time he was nervous. It made him cluck like a chicken.

We better cut up the corpse, one of the men said. It'll be easier that way.

Bennie made a move for the door.

Where you going? said the man in the purple shirt.

I live upstairs, said Bennie. I thought I'd lie down for a while. I work tonight.

You're staying right here. Jack—he turned to the man in the suit—bring the tools.

Bennie needed to sit down, but the mattress was up against the window leaning over the two armchairs. The only other chair was on the opposite side, and he'd have to step over Orlando. He looked at Joey, who shrugged.

Joey, please, he implored him. I don't want to watch this.

I don't either. They'll do it in the bathroom.

But I can hear.

Cover your ears.

The two men carted Orlando's pieces, wrapped in wax paper and tied neatly with butcher string, out of the room. They came back and stood on either side of Bennie and asked again where the money was.

Despite the very real danger he was facing, Bennie kept his composure. He concluded that Mercedes had taken the twenty thousand, but he wasn't about to tell the two men that.

Then Joey saved him. Guys, he said, Bennie don't know anything. He's a stupid Cuban. All he knows is dealing cards. Leave him alone.

The two men looked at each other, then back at Joey. The short one said, We don't take orders from you.

Listen fuck-head, Bennie here doesn't have the money. And if Archie gives you any grief, tell him I answer directly to Meyer and he can go suck a moose.

The men grumbled at Joey and left to drop pieces of Orlando all over the desert. Bennie asked Joey what was going on. Either Joey didn't know or he didn't let on. Later that night, as the two of them shared a six-pack of beer, Bennie asked Joey how he knew those thugs.

I got some juice in this town, Bennie. Me and Meyer grew up on the same block. You can't fuck around with Lansky. He owns everyone in Vegas, including me. He owns you, except you don't know it. Orlando tried to pull a fast one and he paid for it.

What did he do? Bennie asked.

I'd like to know that myself. The whole thing's unsavory, I know, but there's nothing to be done about it. Joey used the word *unsavory* with great delicacy. You sure you don't know anything about that money?

Bennie shook his head.

I have a feeling you do, Joey said. He finished his beer and left.

Bennie didn't see Mercedes for two weeks, and every day of those two weeks one of Archie's men came by asking about the money. Joey's juice was keeping Bennie from the butcher's block. It was the loneliest period of his life. He worked, he ate, he came home, and he sat by the door to his room until it was time for bed. Day in and day out without a holiday, not even Christmas, on which he worked a double shift and made five hundred dollars, but he had nothing to spend it on. He didn't like whores and had no need of a car. He paid twenty dollars a week for his room. His work clothes were provided by the casino, and he had no family to care for, not in Vegas or Miami or Cuba. As he pondered his sorry state, cursing the day he ever decided to leave the island, he heard a knock at his door and Mercedes's plaintive voice asking to be let in.

Where have you been? he asked.

I was in Mexico but I'm back now.

I can see that, he said. What happened between you and Orlando?

He tried a nasty thing on me, ese pinche cabrón.

What? Bennie asked.

I can't say, Mercedes said, suddenly coy.

You didn't have to kill him.

He wouldn't stop. There was a knife there. I just try to scare him but he kept coming and I hit him with it. I just try to scare him.

By now Mercedes had grown very agitated. Her eyes were wide open and her lips were spread into a grimace, like those Mixtec goddesses you see biting into the hearts of men. Hijo de la chingada, she grumbled.

Bennie wanted to shut the door on her and forget she ever existed. What about the money? he asked.

Mercedes was silent for a moment and grew meek, hunching her shoulders downward and looking up at him with beseeching eyes.

I didn't steal it. I found it.

Oh, to be back in Cuba right now, he thought. Communism had to be better than this.

Mujer, are you crazy? You know half of Vegas is looking for you? What did you do with it?

Mercedes was silent.

If you don't return that money to its owners, they're going to grind you up into picadillo. You understand?

Mercedes straightened up and narrowed her eyes. Let me tell you three things, she said: First, the money is hidden; second, I ain't giving it to nobody; third, you are a big pendejo.

Why did you come here? You are incriminating me, he said to her.

I miss you, güerito. I want you to go away with me and we can be rich together.

That's when he took her by the arm, dragged her out of the room, and slammed the door. When he turned around he saw a letter-size white envelope lying on the dresser, which wasn't there before Mercedes's visit. Inside it was a thick stack of one-hundred-dollar bills. He put it back down, sat on the bed, and stared at it, not knowing whether he should flush it down the toilet or simply ignore it as if it were never there. He started thinking of everything he could do with the money. He could buy himself a fancy car. That would draw the women. He could buy a house. That was the smart thing to do. Or he could escape Las Vegas once and for all. Go to Miami, open up a barbershop, run a small book operation on the side, marry a nice criolla who would give him lots of children.

What about Mercedes? After all, she was the one who had killed Orlando and taken the money. She worked hard, the poor woman, doing laundry, cleaning houses, and selling herself when the opportunity availed itself to lonely men like him who lived in cheap motels without a hope in the world. Most of what she made from her labors she sent to her family in México. At least she said she did. Mercedes was foul mouthed and overweight but not a bad sort. If he squinted really hard he could see traces of beautiful María Félix in her features. She killed Orlando in self-defense. How many women would not have done the same? The more he stared at the envelope the more he thought, Mercedes, Mercedes with that singsong Oaxacan accent of hers and hair like black milk and ever-so-dim resemblance to the most beautiful actress of all time.

He called in sick to work and sat on the bed consumed by an idyll he had never before experienced. He let his mind fly, and the twenty thousand became two hundred thousand. He imagined himself in Mexico, owner of a hacienda surrounded by acres and acres of maguey and a distillery bearing his name, Benjamín Rojas, Producer of Fine Tequila. Across the way there would be a stable of black paso fino horses and a field with a herd of gleaming prize zebu cattle that would be the envy of every ranchero in the comarca. He built a whole architecture of fantasy with him at the center: cars, women, presidents, prime ministers, cardinals, all currying his favor. What Mexico needed was a Cuban with balls, coño, who would create an empire of liquor that would rival the great distilleries of the world—Bacardi, Jack Daniels, Hiram Walker.

That's when someone knocked at the door.

Bennie picked up the envelope and stuffed it into the back of his pants. He looked through the peephole and saw that it was Joey.

Jesus, Joey said as he walked into Bennie's room. It's freezing in here. You'd figure Cuba was in Siberia the way you guys like the cold.

It's on its way there, Bennie said.

Joey sat on the bed and lit up a Cuban Churchill, every puff of smoke round and sweet and perfect.

You have the money, Joey said. As a matter of fact, I'm willing to bet my left testicle you have it on your person even as we speak.

Bennie felt his throat tightening. He sat on the armchair, took out a handkerchief, and blew his nose. The cigar was getting to him.

Joey blew a puff of smoke toward the ceiling. You fucking Cubans can sure make cigars, he said. It's about the only thing you're good at. Twenty grand is pocket change for Meyer, but he hates to be swindled. Why don't you give me the money, spare yourself?

Bennie hesitated. All those dreams of women and paso finos and thousands of acres of maguey plantings going up with Joey's smoke. He reached behind him and handed Joey the envelope.

I'll make you a deal, Bennie, Joey said. I keep fifteen and I'll give you five. Call it a reward for a job well done. Just between you and me. Nobody else has to know.

Joey counted out five thousand and passed them back to Bennie, who took the money without hesitation and put it in his pocket. As he did so he felt his blood thicken and his heart slow a few beats.

After Joey left, Bennie pulled the shades shut and lay on the bed. He tried to summon up his fantasies but all he could think of was the money in his pocket. What was fat Mercedes to him, anyway, and Orlando with that eggplant face of his? Five thousand wasn't twenty but it was enough for a down payment on a small house. The wife and the book operation would come eventually. So would the juice. He didn't realize it then but a spot in his heart had turned to stone.

STORYTELLER

Mama died first. She caught cold. Coughed all night, gave a few heavy sighs, and was silent. I heard, then didn't hear, her from my bed but didn't get up because I knew her time had come. The time for what? That time. That time. I turned over, put the pillow over my head. Papa yelled, sick in bed and his bowels burning. He was no help. Nothing I could do. Nothing I wanted to do.

I fell back asleep, then woke. I had a vision of a man in white who came to my room with a bucket full of fish, wanting me to cook them. I asked why. He said he was hungry. I rose from the bed and took the bucket to the kitchen. I cleaned the fish, remembering the way I'd been taught by Cornelia, scraping away at the scales, then slicing open the belly and pulling out the guts. The process seemed endless; there were enough fish to feed a large crowd. The man in white became my father. I told him to get back in bed to calm his bowels, the same bed Mama lay in. Daily she got quieter; her skin felt like wet ashes. When she was alive it was all bitter. Never liked being alive. She tried to kill me. She tried to burn me out of her womb.

That's too much power for stories, keeping people alive against their will, she said once. Papa never thought that way. He was happy to hear them. Doctor said it was terminal, Port Authority terminal, and Papa taking the outbound bus. That's when he went to bed. To wait, he said. Once death catches up to you, no use running to the next room. Her tentacles are long, like the giant squid in *Twenty Thousand Leagues Under the Sea*. Captain Nemo and all his dignity and madness. They're not long enough for me yet. I know the sun when it hits the window and goes through the glass. Warmth on my skin, then it gets beasty eyed and wants to play. I never did—play, that is, except at chess.

Mama's crossed the threshold. Papa went along with it, not wanting to contradict her. That would only have brought her wild tongue on him, poor man, poor man, his guts twisting against themselves. But he's as happy she's gone as I am. Not that he's ever said so; he just hasn't said otherwise.

When I washed Mama in the morning she was cold and stiff. Some people turn like that after years of vitriol. I read in a book—I read everything that reaches my hands and eyes, such as they are—that if you put a mirror under someone's nose and it doesn't fog up, that person's dead. I couldn't find a mirror small enough. I looked in the kitchen, and I looked in Mama's chest of drawers—perhaps there I might find a powder case or small vanity. I looked in the living room for the silver tray Papa had given her for their twenty-fifth anniversary. Cleaning lady stole that, as she'd taken everything of value in the house, even the sex videos Papa would watch when Mama wasn't home and he thought I was sleeping or reading. Just because I'm blind doesn't mean I'm deaf. Finally, when I'd just about given up and resigned myself to never knowing for sure if Mama had died or was just in a deep sleep, I remembered the round makeup mirror in the bathroom. I brought that and held it under her nose. The mirror didn't fog, not the least, and there was no question after that. She'd been dead, dead for some time. I didn't tell Papa, thinking, What's the use? He'll find out soon enough. So I told him a story, a good long one about a university professor, one of our neighbors, who falls in love with a much younger professor. The young professor is horrified and flees from the older professor, leaving him alone and in despair. After the story Papa's belly began to hurt worse than before and he asked for the heating pad and the painkillers and cursed me for telling him such a tragic story. He wanted something happy to counteract the sadness of that other one. I reminded him I only told one story a day—my mind wasn't up for more—and promised I'd give him what he wanted the following day.

No sex, though, he said. That only gets me worked up and there's nothing I can do about it.

I said, No sex.

And no death.

I said, No death.

And no solitude.

That I couldn't promise, considering that's all I knew, as did he, who was about to die.

I spent the rest of the day trying to devise a story that had no solitude, no death, and no sex. No sex? It was like fishing for the impossible fish.

I read books of stories, books on the crafting of stories, books about mythology and legend. I told him the story of Perseus and Medusa, which he said rightly that I stole, and the story of Baucis and Philemon, which he found dull. I also told him the stories of Peleus, of Penelope and the suitors, and Agamemnon and Clytemnestra, but he was unimpressed by these and said perhaps I should stick to telling my own. I then told him one about a man getting out of Cuba on a boat, taking extreme care in composing it to suit his demands. I don't know if I succeeded or failed. He never said.

The next morning, after a sleepless night, I made my way to his bedroom. I gave Papa his coffee and moved over to Mama's side of the bed. She, being dead, had not moved. I looked closely into her face, saw wrinkles and blotches here and there on the cheeks and forehead. Her eyes had lost their color. I could barely distinguish the iris from the white. Her nose, that fine sharp thing that resembled a shark's dorsal fin, had sunk somewhat and turned bonier than it used to be. Her belly had grown overnight, so she looked pregnant as she must have looked with me. I'd never known a dead person before. I had no way of telling that these were the first steps in the process of decomposition: the formation of liquid materials inside the body as a result of the breakdown of flesh through the action of intestinal bacteria and the production of vapors.

Papa said she'd been snoring all night. I was mortified—allow me the pun. How was I to know then that the dead fill up with gas, which causes all manner of sounds as it escapes the body through its major orifices, the alpha and omega, the burp and fart, the wheeze and flutter. *Rigor mortis, livor mortis, algor mortis.* Then the body falls apart. The stench is unbearable. She bloated up, then bloated down. I put aside my feelings and finished washing her nevertheless, as I was compelled to do in order to keep Papa from being suspicious, her skin rubbery to the touch and cool, like ice cream that has lain outside the refrigerator long enough to start melting.

Sometimes I think I live on two planes simultaneously. The first is the plane where everything exists in relation to my nonsight. Someone might say, Sure, he's blind as a bat, but that statement merely cloaks reality in the flat inaccuracy of cliché. I am not blind; I am not a bat. I see things through the blear of shadow, a featureless gouache. At night, a light becomes a dispersal of yellow, the color of urine, the consistency of engine oil. I glop through. I turn on the radio, and there is the second plane, of sound. Music blooms riding the shallows of the bed where I lie, then dips into the depths, a ship coming into port, a street full of people walking, chatting, or encased in their individual silences, a woman waiting for a taxi, a man buying a newspaper at the entrance to the subway. I merely follow the music again and again, sometimes to the park after it snows and children are sledding; other times to a funeral where a family's in wake for a five-year-old child who broke her neck in a fall. I make up what I see, not the other way around.

Often there are the feet of women, so different from Mama's gnarled, bunioned ones, and I imagine what I'd do in bed with a woman, where and how I'd start, how much time I'd spend on the breasts, the belly, the hairy muff between her legs, before moving to the feet. I think about my blood father and my mother and how they conceived me. Was it merely the quick release of sperm into the vagina, or did they take their time, touching here, licking there? Did they feel the surge inside them, like an ocean wanting to get out? Or was it more beastly, quick mount and dismount, then off to the hunt? Were they shepherds or barbarians? They had animal horns, shofars, shells letting out a boastful note or two like the blaring mastodons. They had reed flutes, sweet, simple, one scale, one key. They didn't require much. A thin melodic line can take you a long way. It can lead to pasture, it can bring you to water, can settle you down at night, and raise you in the morning.

My mama was dead, my papa didn't know, and I was to make happy stories to make him happy, move off melody, groove into harmony. Sleep became impossible. I lay in bed in the fluid darkness thinking of what I would tell, how I would tell it. Papa, be happy. All through the telling I heard a cornet coming from the street corner, music man making what he makes best, the barbarian and the shepherd shaping their breath into song.

JOHNNY LUNA'S SEVEN TRIES

On September 23, 1995, Johnny Luna settled into the bow of the *Ana María,* a twenty-foot launch he built for the voyage, and took his last look at the city of Havana, illuminated dimly by the first rays of dawn. It was Johnny's seventh attempt at crossing the Straits of Florida, and having consulted a babalawo in Arroyo Arenas, he was certain that the *Ana María* would land him, if not in Miami, then somewhere along the Florida Keys, where he could claim his right to political asylum. He had spent six months in jail after his previous attempt when the raft he'd put together had fallen apart in rough water three miles from shore, and he and his two companions were forced to swim back, landing on the Malecón just as a patrol drove by. If he failed again, he was certain that the authorities would make him rot in jail. That's why he had consulted the babalawo and paid a hefty amount, in dollars, for a Russian outboard motor that sputtered and smoked whenever he started it but otherwise ran beautifully.

Despite the care he took in building the boat from plans left behind by his grandfather, Alepo Rodríguez, the great shark fisherman who had been swallowed by the waves off Jaimanitas in 1952, and despite the babalawo's blessing, none of the friends he approached would join him. Johnny had acquired a reputation as a salao, a fellow forever mired in the salt of bad luck, and crossing the Florida Straits was a serious matter. If the storms and sharks didn't get you, the Coast Guard would, and they'd put you in the same jail cell with a gang of pederasts. At least two of those friends spread the news, and when Fefa Manguera, the head of the neighborhood defense committee, heard that El Salao was at it again, she gave a big, raucous laugh but didn't bother reporting Johnny to the higher-ups or paying a visit to his mother to ask the usual impertinent questions. Only Obdulio Martínez, the dim-witted teenage son of a garbage collector who lived down the street, agreed to accompany Johnny.

Johnny ignored the neighbors' sly half smiles as he walked by, the occasional shout, "Bacalao salao," coming from one of the balconies overhead, and went about his business with the aplomb of a seasoned sailor. Mornings he waited in the rationing line to get whatever food he and his mother were entitled to—split peas one day, dry mackerel the next. On a good day they might have some meat or a ham hock, or a half pound of rice. Afternoons he'd go to his aunt's house in Lawton to meet up with the cheese man or the egg man or the pork man. Black-market vendors required dollars, and if he didn't have any, he'd simply head in the direction of the Malecón and walk along the sea wall, looking at the ocean as it stretched all the way to the horizon and beyond, where the Promised Land lay. Everyone was leaving the island. Why couldn't he? He was home by six usually, when his mother served him a bowl of watery split-pea soup or, on bad days, a mayonnaise sandwich and a glass of sugared water. After eight o'clock, when his mother went to sleep, he'd leave the house again and walk through the streets of Havana, never taking the same route twice in a row, to the old garage where his uncle Berto hid his 1956 Chrysler Imperial, waiting for the day when the revolution was finally over and he could drive it proudly down the street like the old-fashioned capitalist he fancied himself to be. The garage was about forty feet deep and the Chrysler was all the way in the rear, up on blocks and quietly rusting away. In the front, unbeknownst to anyone but Obdulio the dimwit, Johnny would work through the night building the *Ana María*, a boat so sturdy nothing but the most extreme act of God would sink it, and even then, Johnny would think while taking a cigarette break, the Old Man would have a real struggle on his hands.

And so, Johnny became a creature of the night. Often he could hear, or thought he could hear, a faint murmur settling over the crumbling city after midnight. Off in the distance a dog barked or a radio played; outside the garage two lovers spoke.

My love, did you bring the banana?

Yes, darling. Here it is. For you.

Johnny listened to them while Obdulio slept in the backseat of the Chrysler and salivated, whether from lust or old hunger he didn't know. All conversations in Cuba devolved into matters of food.

Give it to me, Papi.

Johnny dropped the hammer he was holding against a metal bucket and made a loud noise. Obdulio woke with a start.

¿Qué pasó? he said, sitting up and looking through the rear window.

Nothing. Go back to sleep, Johnny answered and kept on working until his eyes closed involuntarily and he dreamed of Miami Beach nightclubs and gorgeous tanned women with large, shapely breasts.

Johnny, it must be said, had a wife, but she was one of those women who consider sex an unpleasant marital duty to be performed twice monthly without abandon or fanfare, like getting an injection. During the three years they were married, Johnny's wife had grown dull and morose, feeling betrayed that Johnny had not made good on his promise to get her pregnant. She was subject to fits of resentment that took the form of burning Johnny's coffee so that it became undrinkable or salting his food to such a degree that he had to spit it out. When she finally went to live with her sister in Cotorro, Johnny was ecstatic. In fact, he celebrated that night by drinking a bottle of rum and running the Russian motor until it whined and rattled.

Mayami, Mayami, Mayami is so good, Mayami, Mayami, Mayami, come to me, Johnny chanted, dancing around Obdulio, who hooted and leaped like a warrior about to wrestle a lion.

In six months the *Ana María* was finished, and it was such an exemplary picture of a seagoing vessel that Johnny entertained the thought of selling her for a thousand dollars and staying in Havana until that son-of-a-bitch Fidel died. With a thousand dollars he could fix up his uncle's Chrysler. With a thousand dollars he could approach that girl with the long legs and jet-black hair who lived on the corner of Manrique and Lagunas Streets and call up to her, Come on, sugar, let's take a drive around the city. With a thousand dollars he'd be a big man in this godforsaken city. But those thoughts stayed with him only two nights. By God, he said to himself on the third night, I'll make it to La Yuma or die. With a renewed sense of purpose he went off to Santa Fe, the little fishing village in the outskirts of Havana, to observe what time the Coast Guard patrols passed by, and he did so for two weeks, hiding behind a stand of sea grape, swatting at mosquitoes and recording the times on an old school notebook.

Rather than tell his mother directly, he decided he would leave a letter for her to read, reassuring her that he would send for her as soon as he was settled. She still loved El Comandante as she had loved Johnny's father, who disappeared for weeks at a time, showing up to take her money and beat her up. Fidel is the most wonderful man in the world, she would say raising her eyes to the ceiling. After reading the letter, his mother would cry for a day, then go downstairs to gossip with the neighborhood ladies and forget about her son. At least this is what he told himself.

In preparation for the voyage, he had been gathering provisions, buying some, borrowing others, and, when he had no other choice, stealing the rest. In the forward compartment of the *Ana María* he stowed five jugs of water, several bags of stale bread, a block of farmer's cheese, and seven cans of sardines. Along the sides of the boat he placed a stolen flashlight, two oars he had borrowed from his uncle, a fishing line with several hooks and sinkers that Obdulio's father had given them, an old knife from his mother's kitchen, a compass and an ancient sextant, both stolen from the naval museum in La Cabaña, and one hundred liters of gasoline that had cost him several hundred dollars. Also on the boat, well hidden from view for now, was a small American flag he hoped to wave once he got within view of La Yuma. In a frivolous moment he decided to take the leather seat of the Chrysler, cracked and brittle with age, and glued it amidships with marine epoxy so that Obdulio could sleep comfortably on the way across.

At midnight of the appointed day, Johnny and Obdulio waited for Obdulio's father, Manolo, to arrive with the garbage truck he had commandeered to transport the *Ana María* to the little cove in Santa Fe. At twelve thirty Johnny grew worried; at one o'clock he was desperate. At one fifteen Obdulio's father finally showed up, not in the twenty-five-footer with a canvas cover he had promised, but in a small Moskvitch pickup with a six-foot bed. Johnny's heart sank several levels. He sat on the front fender of the Chrysler and felt tears welling in his eyes, but he contained them.

Manolo, Johnny said to Obdulio's father. How are we going to load a fifteen-foot boat on that cockroach?

Don't worry, asere, Manolo said. We'll do it. I brought enough rope so we can tie it securely on top. No problem.

Obdulio's father was determined to have his son in the United States so he could send remittances home.

What are people going to think when they see a Moskvitch with a boat twice its size tied on top?

Nothing, asere, said Manolo. Because there isn't anybody out at this time of night. You think this is Nueva York?

I thought you were going to bring a big truck, Johnny said, thinking of the two lovers for no reason in particular.

Asere, what happened is somebody else took it for the night. But don't worry so much. This is going to work. You'll see.

It took the three of them an hour to load and tie the *Ana María* onto the Moskvitch. Johnny thought for sure the shock absorbers would give way, but he was wrong. The pickup merely lurched and groaned and finally settled nicely six inches from the ground. The *Ana María* lay upside down, its prow extending six feet beyond the cab and blocking all but a six-inch band of windshield. Manolo reassured Johnny that he could drive the streets of Havana with his eyes closed. Given that in those days the government shut down the city's electric power at night in order to save money, that's pretty much what they'd have to do: drive in the dark with the headlights turned off.

One pothole and there goes the front axle, Johnny said.

Manolo once again tried to calm him, then reached under the driver's seat and pulled out a bottle of homemade firewater that he passed to Johnny. Johnny took a swig and gave it back to Manolo.

That's for the trip, Manolo said, pushing the bottle away. Make sure you make an offering to Yemayá before you push off.

They drove in silence and darkness without hitting a single pothole and reached the turnoff at 2:45 AM, with plenty of time to ship out by 3:27 when the next patrol was due. As Manolo negotiated the sandy road that led to the cove, the Moskvitch waddled and almost tipped over a couple of times, then hit a rut, where the wheels spun themselves into the sand and lost traction.

Manolo hit the steering wheel with the palm of his hand. Johnny cursed God and all the angels, and both left the cab simultaneously, walking around the truck to gauge how deeply the tires were imbedded in the sand. Manolo dug around the two front tires while Johnny stood by the passenger door and looked at Obdulio, who was sleeping soundly inside. What he wouldn't give to sleep like that! He was already resigning himself to going back to the garage to wait for another day when Manolo stood upright and proclaimed that they would have to take the boat off the Moskvitch. Then he would let some air out of the tires and that would do the trick. Easy, Manolo said. Easy? Johnny thought. Nothing had ever been easy for him.

Suddenly he sensed someone next to him, and when he looked to his right he saw a round, bristled face looking up at him. Johnny's blood turned cold and the back of his neck tensed up.

Señor, what's the problem? The man was being overly formal, given the circumstances.

Nada, answered Johnny, too nervous to say anything else.

The man looked at the truck's wheels sunk halfway in the sand, then back up at Johnny.

It looks like something to me.

Soon Manolo joined them and asked the man what he was doing there at such an hour.

172

The same thing you're doing, trying to get off this shitty island.

He led them on a path through a stand of sea grape to the water, where a boat, or what passed for a boat, was waiting to shove off. The man called to two others who were helping some women and their children on board, and between the five of them—Obdulio remained blissfully asleep—they were able to unload the *Ana María* and drag it on the sand to the water's edge. The three men were impressed by Johnny's launch and wanted to tie it to their ramshackle vessel, an old wooden boat that had no motor but a sail made out of two bed sheets sewn together. Four empty oil barrels, fastened on either side, kept the vessel from sinking. Johnny said no. We have women and children with us, a man complained. He made a threatening move in Johnny's direction but Manolo intervened, thanking them for their help and offering the men two jugs of water and three cans of sardines for their efforts. They took the offer and went back to their boat, but not before the short man who had first approached them said to Johnny, Who do you think you are? This is a socialist country.

Johnny waited until the other vessel was well out to sea and out of his sight before pushing the *Ana María* into the water. She bobbed a few times; then her prow settled squarely against the waves. She was a good boat, he thought proudly. He and Obdulio took their leave of Manolo, who stood on the shore with his shoulders hunched and his large hands dangling helplessly at his sides. Johnny heard him crying and assured him that his son would soon be sending a thousand dollars home every month. Manolo's weeping grew more pronounced; then it stopped altogether. After feeling the bottom with his hands to check for leaks and finding it dry as bone, Johnny helped Obdulio on board and climbed in after him. Obdulio waved at the darkness where he had last seen his father and sat on the leather car seat, giddy with anticipation.

Once the *Ana María* was in deep enough, Johnny lowered the Russian outboard into the water, opened the throttle, and gave a yank of the starter rope. The motor sputtered and died. Johnny yanked several times, each time pulling harder than the last until he was out of breath. Stupid Russians! They can't even build a good motor. No wonder the Soviet Union fell apart. Then he heard a dim voice through the gloom, *Ta hogao*. It's flooded. Let it rest. At first he thought it was Manolo; then he realized it was Obdulio's voice, which was like his father's but younger and rougher. Johnny found the bottle of firewater wedged under the seat and spilled some on the water as an offering before taking a drink. He offered the bottle to Obdulio, who refused, saying, Eso eh'el diablo. Now he sounded less like his father and more like Bola de Nieve, the singer. After listening to the water lap the sides of the boat for what seemed an eternity, Johnny tried again. The motor coughed and started, releasing a burst of burned-oil smoke that, to Johnny, smelled like the perfume of his dreams.

Hold on, Obdulio, he said and revved the engine as high as it would go. The *Ana María* lurched, gained speed, and was soon skimming the flat sea like a flying fish.

It was about two miles out that Johnny turned and looked back at Havana. From that distance the city looked like a mirage, nestled in a soft gray light that made it float over the sea, over the land, over all material things. It was the most beautiful sight he had ever seen. Havana was the world to him, heaven and hell and purgatory combined, and he understood that he was leaving it behind for good. Even as he was reaching this realization he started turning the boat around until it was pointing back to shore. Obdulio sat calmly at first, like a prince enjoying a ride on his private launch, and slowly he became aware of what Johnny was doing.

No, no, he said. Coño, ¡no!

Johnny woke from his reverie and headed back north. When he reached the approximate spot of the first turning, he remembered his mother, whom he had abandoned. This time he slowed down the boat and made a broader arc, and when the city came into view, Obdulio said, I want to go to La Yuma, his overgrown child's voice cracking. Johnny kept turning until the boat completed a full circle. This time he thought of the girl on the balcony with the pearly skin and beautiful black hair. How could he abandon those delights? Now Obdulio was screaming and it sounded to Johnny like a high-speed circular saw cutting through a dry log. He turned again. The *Ana María* circled six times. Every time Johnny thought of someone or something he was leaving, he pointed her in the direction of Havana; then hearing Obdulio's scream over the sound of the motor, he turned the boat northward. As he was about to circle yet one more time, the sun appeared over the eastern horizon, red and massive, spreading its rays until the sea, the city, and the sky grew indistinct and they were suspended in a blaze so pure and ubiquitous it was directionless. Johnny screamed louder than Obdulio, louder than the Russian motor, and passed the point of his turning, weeping for what he had left behind and racing full speed ahead into the future.

EATING PIG

When Angel was alone, which was all too often, it was memory that brought him to the feasts of his childhood. Always there was a pig and always a man cooking it in the backyard, hired for the purpose. The cook drank rum from the moment he arrived at dawn, and he had the same name, Joaquín. It took all day (no way to fast-cook pork, especially on the bone) so that the pig would be ready by five. Always it was sunny and Angel was surrounded by cousins, mostly older, some younger, whom he liked in varying degrees based on their ability to allay the loneliness he dreaded even then. The men played cards in the *bohío*. His aunts and his two grandmothers cooked huge pots of pig's feet and tripe. Many memories or one memory repeated with variations around the pig, spread-eagled over the coals and Joaquín basting, always basting, the pig skin crackling, sweating out the fat that dribbled to the fire, making it sputter and flame. Its eyes half-closed, its eyelashes wispy and dreamful, its snout curling upward as it cooked. Joaquín usually kept the head. The cheeks are the best part, he'd say, taking a bite.

Angel did not remember the taste, or what happened afterward, whether people left or stayed for days, whether the scene was a permanent state or a temporary condition. Ser or estar. Heaven or hell. Beyond that day there were bombs exploding all around the city, torturers torturing, corpses on street corners, mouths full of ants, mothers weeping, fathers wailing. Always was not always. Family members leaving, family members left behind, some in prison, some outside. The island itself a prison, the smell of tropical rot floating over the grass, the trees. The white sand of the beaches and the sun the only permanence. Forget the feast and the family, forget the dancing and the card playing. His grandmother dreamed of being a bird, his mother of being a fish. No one dreamed of being a worm, but that's what they all became, burrowing into the dung heap, then trying to burrow out. Eating pig, is there anything as fulsome and healthy? The moment, the cooking, the weeping, the wailing, the memory, the memory.

THE QUEEN OF
THE MALEⒸÓN

You left no stone unturned, wanting so to be part of a history that denied you, made you puny to the point of disappearance. He who left is always leaving, they told you. He who is silent doesn't know the limits of his isolation. What? you asked. They provided no clean answer, no certain way for you to accept their neglect. History is like that: You leave through the door of exile and you won't ever know, will you, how your life would have turned out. It's your problem. Nobody else's.

The truth: After thirty-eight years nothing is left of you there. The lie: that you have any claim to that place, that culture, that language. The in-between: the big city that offered you respite. There it didn't matter how you acted or dressed, what you said in what language, when you came or went, what rough beast lay inside you waiting to be born. The women didn't care;

the bosses who hired you didn't. But you had to leave the big city, and once you started leaving you couldn't stop. Off you went into another exile and then into another narrower one, and to yet a smaller one until all you could do to get through the needle's eye was disappear, leaving behind no trace, not in the towns you visited, not in the places where you lived, not in the children you fathered. Your friends quickly forgot you. Your lovers went off into the realms of matrimony, divorce, depression. In a few years no one ever heard of you, not in the cities of your exile, not in the island of your birth. You were a breeze, a wisp; you were a molecule bouncing back and forth in the ether. You were the ether. No one.

Nearing the age of fifty, you resolved that if you didn't return immediately, you never would and so you did. In the city of your birth you stayed with a third cousin, the only family remaining, all the rest having died or left the island. Nine days of no feeling, of a stone lodged in your gut, of throwing yourself into the waters of the past and sinking into tropical darkness. What could you do? You walked Havana from north to south and east to west finding no solace. You recognized many things but were welcomed nowhere. Rum, lots of it. You were a ghost. No. You were a cartoon, healthy and well fed, lacking nothing in your life you couldn't buy. Even breathing was difficult.

Then you met Tania, the queen of the Malecón, who walked like the waves and laughed like the wind. She had a glorious body and the eyes of a blackbird. One look was enough. She licked her lips and they glistened with the sunlight coming off the water. She needed no jewelry, she told you, just money.

She'd do anything for money. Still, you bought a bracelet from a man by the cathedral, made of God-knows-what metal the seller swore was gold. She wore it for two days and then no more. What happened to it? you asked. I sold it. Five dollars, she said. I paid fifty. Bobo. You know what I can do with fifty dollars? Next time give me the money.

You were ready to offer her anything. You had three more days. You didn't want to leave, afraid that all that Tania gave you would evaporate, and she would take up with someone else who'd give her more, take her places, make her feel like the world was bigger than the miserable island she was trapped on. And leave for what, the disappearing act, the exile inside the exile inside the exile?

You have to be either very brave or very stupid to stay in a country everyone else is dying to leave, and you were neither. The sense of being watched was real. It was she, you found out, who went to state security and let them know what you did and didn't do. I hooked a writer, she must have said. She insisted you go to the hotel room in the Nacional, the one with the beautiful view and the hidden cameras. Now your lovemaking is in the state security archives. How many men had Tania lured into that sordid trap? What did she gain by it? Money, of course.

The lie, the truth: When you received a copy of the tape in the mail, you didn't have the will to be outraged. It was grainy and poorly lit and showed two people, one obviously you (they made sure your face was clearly in focus and your voice audible, especially when you moaned), engaged in mostly normal missionary coitus. Only your unusual interest in Tania's feet might be cause for concern. The archivists were disappointed at not finding anything more lurid than that. Still, they sent it as a warning to stop writing against the government. They could have arrested you while you were on the island, but you weren't important enough. Your articles never made it to the mainstream media. You put the tape behind some books and forgot about it, something you couldn't quite get yourself to do with Tania, the queen of the Malecón. Ten years later you returned, promising yourself not to look for her, but after a fitful night in the hotel that brought back too many memories, too much longing, you went in search of her. A family of six were living in her old apartment, a tiny room in a cuartería in Centro Habana. None of them knew Tania. They'd taken the apartment after the previous tenant, an old lady who'd been rich before the revolution, was found dead on the rickety bed. They had to wash the apartment with kerosene to get rid of the stench.

THE DEATH OF CHANO POZO

Chano Pozo was the greatest rumbero who ever lived. He could play in one rhythm, sing in another, and dance in a third. People would go see him at La Conga or the Spotlite and listen and watch and be converted: Chano Pozo was good, but even the good can be better, and sometimes they can be the best. In music you can't be the best all the time—everyone knows that. Sometimes your head isn't right or your spirit has crawled up a tree and refuses to be coaxed down. Sometimes—it's that simple—you had too much stuff the night before and you can't play what the music demands of you. But when it happens you can blow the roof off the place and send the audience into orbit. With Chano it happened so frequently people thought he could call a saint to mount him at will and then he'd be off, racing into the forest, his hands turned white

183

from the speed and complexity of the rhythms. When he came out of the forest, he was on the edge of life itself, and his eyes, if you looked at them directly, were lit by Changó's lightning. Possessed, con el santo encima, as they say, Chano was like a horse. For hours he raced up and down mountains, across endless plains, into a night so thick only the saints could enter.

A few days before the feast of Changó, Chano dreamed that a panther was about to bite his neck. In the dream was a sound of someone laughing. Across the street the beasts of the forest were pacing back and forth, contained by the dense vegetation that divides the past from the present. The forest is a fearful place. Everything bad happens there, and everything good, too, though many times you cannot tell for years. If you make a million dollars, is it good or bad? And if you find a good woman? And if you cut a man's throat because he dishonored you? Only the saints know beforehand, and they won't reveal the truth easily. Chano could hear the roar of the beasts and he could hear their bodies as they moved through the foliage.

The panther came after Changó had left Chano and gone back to his lair in the forest. The beast stood over Chano's body, looking at him with yellow eyes, hungry but leery of biting flesh as black as his. When he woke, the panther leaped through the window. Next to him Cacha was sleeping soundly. He got up, walked over to the window, opened it, and looked down at the snow-covered sidewalk. A set of human footprints led from one end of the street to the other, then disappeared around the corner into the empty avenue. Chano lit a cigarette and watched the snow come down, heavy and white like wet cotton. Nothing like this in Havana, nothing this white or pretty.

He couldn't remember playing the drums last night, but he knew he had from the tingling in his fingers and the rhythms filling his head like thunder inside trunks of hollow trees.

No, it wasn't thunder, it was the heart beating inside Cacha's chest—*cu-bop, cu-bop.* That's what he heard all the time now, whether he was uptown or downtown, whether he was playing or sleeping or eating or making love to another woman. It was Cacha in his ears, in his head, in his blood. She'd told him the same thing happened to her: She could hear his playing, she could feel his hands on her skin no matter where she was.

When he was finished smoking, Chano flicked the butt toward the snow and went back to bed. He needed the rest. That night he had a gig at La Conga, but first he had to find El Cabito, the dealer who'd sold him the bad weed, and square with him. He didn't want that bad energy lingering while he played. The panther appeared three more times, and each time Chano woke, distraught and confused, wondering what it meant: bad or good? Snow came down more thickly and no cars passed, no one was out. Asleep he'd heard the panther make a deep purr, then the panting again that smelled like raw meat. In one dream the cat had placed its paw on the bed and sniffed around his throat, and still in the dream Chano invoked Yemayá, saint of the sea, and the beast moved away into the depths of the forest so that he could see only its yellow eyes.

Of course there's a forest in Cubop City. It's everywhere, and every tree, every creature has a santo, an orisha, if you prefer the Yoruba name, even that stunted tree surrounded by dog shit that grows outside your building. The moon has a santo, the sun has a santo, the cockroach scurrying across the floor of your living room is a santo's snack. The santos eat them like pork cracklings, then smack their lips. Remember that the next time you step on one.

Around noon that day, after Cacha left the house, Chano finally roused himself from bed, got dressed, and went to La Palma for breakfast. It had stopped snowing and the sun was out, but the temperature had gone down to the single digits and the wind blew down the avenue like a train. The heat inside counters the cold outside, he always said to his friends, but that maxim didn't keep his ears from stinging on his walk to the restaurant.

He sat at his favorite seat, the middle stool at the counter, and asked Simón, the cook, if he'd seen El Cabito around, but Simón avoided a direct answer, figuring he wasn't in this world to inform on people's whereabouts but to cook their food. In the case of Chano it was two fried eggs, a large slice of pressed Cuban bread with butter, and a café con leche with three sugars. A side order of ripe plantains. Like a South American. That's what he liked.

A lot of people come around here, Simón said. They like my cooking.

When? Chano asked.

I know there's trouble between you two. Why should I tell you?

Chano gave a quick laugh that didn't hide his anger. El Cabito cheated me, he said. I'm not going to let him get away with that.

You're a hothead, Simón said. Forget it.

If you weren't so old, I'd break your neck for saying that.

Go ahead and break it, Simón said. You'd do me a favor.

As Chano ate, the panther came back, blacker and more threatening than in his dream. This time it was behind him and had its front paws on his shoulders trying to push him down. Chano straightened his back and said a prayer to Changó. Still, he was bothered that a dream animal had made its way into reality and was now stalking him. Maybe it was a message from the spirit world to slow down, become a son of Obatalá, the saint of the north, and be virtuous, eat rice pudding, drink coconut milk.

Just as Chano was finishing, Juan Pedro walked in and sat next to him. Juan Pedro was a braggart and a dandy, but Chano tolerated him because they'd both grown up in Cayo Hueso, the Havana neighborhood that was so tough not even the police dared to enter. It was that neighborhood Chano carried inside and Juan Pedro had the habit of reminiscing about those days. Remember *Chicho el viejo* who used to walk backward? And the crazy woman who lived on the upstairs floor, screaming for the death of the dictator Machado? Remember the boy who called you maricón and you beat him up so bad you almost killed him? Chano remembered. He was eight years old and the boy was three years older and a head taller. Dropped him with a combination hook and upper cut. When the boy went down, Chano kicked him in the face, the ribs, the groin. Chano would have killed him had not a man pulled him away. The boy stood and Chano noticed the tears coming out of his eyes, the snot smeared on his cheeks, and shame trembling on his lips. It was almost like sex, seeing the boy like that. Chano tried to break free of the man and go at him again, but the grip was strong, and the santo had already dismounted. The fight led to the first of many stays at the boys' reformatory. Nobody called him maricón again. Once you enter the forest, you can't leave, not for long.

Chano asked Juan Pedro about Cabito. Juan Pedro told him there was a three-day party at Mama Mandinga's place. Chano was sure to find him there, selling weed.

Chano paid his bill and walked into the biting wind of the avenue. He tried to warm himself by thinking of his mother's bed. While she was out earning a living, he'd get under the covers and smell the lilac cologne she wore after her bath, which lingered in the sheets mixed with her own womanly scent. Many afternoons he spent hiding there, watching the shadows lengthen and the dark gather at the corners until he heard the front door open and her voice calling him. He was not one given to nostalgia, but on frigid days like this he was frustrated with the life he had and wanted a different one, a nice apartment downtown, a house in Havana, lots of money and a brand-new Cadillac—un Colepato. He could have that life if he kept playing his drums, making his music. Eventually he could get his own band, like Machito and Dizzy and Cugat.

In those days Mama Mandinga held parties in her house and charged a cover. It was a way of making a little money, a way of keeping the spirits up. There was a live band and lots of liquor and food, but the people came for the dancing, which went on from the moment Mama opened the door till she threw the last partiers out. By the time Chano got there, there were five couples left and the band had stopped playing, except the guitarist, who was strumming the chords to a bolero. Jeva music, Chano called it, not in a derogatory way. Women like boleros. A bolero is a perfect way to end a party if you score. If not, that music can crawl inside you and make you miserable.

Mama was sitting in the foyer, her haunches spilling over the sides of a wooden folding chair, and she greeted Chano like a prodigal son. She refused to take his money. Mama wanted Chano to get to the drums and play a set to send her clients on a happy note, but Chano refused, saying he didn't want to waste himself. He told her he was looking for El Cabito. Mama misunderstood, thinking Chano wanted drugs, and scrunched her face, her lower lip curling around a curse word she decided to keep to herself. She looked down briefly at the cigar box where she kept her money. No one but Mama touched that box.

He was here yesterday afternoon, she said. Sat on the couch talking. You know how he is, like he owns the world. Then he started dealing and I told him to leave. Here, in my house, you don't do drugs. You hear, Chano? Cabito's no good. Don't trust a man with a gold tooth.

Chano reminded Mama he himself had two.

Two is not one, she said.

She picked up her cigar box and stood slowly. She was a big woman, made bigger by the loose housedress she wore. Se acabó lo que se daba. Party's over. I'm going to bed. Be careful. El Cabito was in the war. He killed a lot of men. Oggún, the saint of weapons, is on his side.

I'm a son of Changó, Chano said.

That saint is fickle.

Chano gave a quick laugh. He'd never been afraid of anyone in his life, and when you're unafraid you have every weapon at your disposal. There was a nice-looking mulata, whose boyfriend was smoking reefer out on the street. She smiled at him. That was the boyfriend's fault. You never left a beautiful woman like that at a party like this, especially when Chano was around. He was devoted to women and he had the talk. Chano was tempted but he didn't bite.

There was one more place he could check tonight, El Río Café, but that was way uptown and the cold was getting to him. His teeth were chattering and the wind went right through the lined gabardine with a leather collar he'd bought more for style than warmth. He needed to return to his apartment to warm up and rest before his gig.

When he got there Cacha was gone. Instead he found the panther again, panting like a bellow. Chano took off his shoes, which were wet and stained along the sides with dried salt, and lay on the bed. Tonight he wanted to smoke those drums, get them talking the language of the forest and make sure Cacha heard it in midtown, where she'd gone with her friends. That woman could move her hips to the music like Ochún, the saint of romance and flirtation. She had skin the color of honey and golden eyes, and Chano loved her the first time he saw her. For a long time he tried to get her to come with him, but she refused because he had a woman back in Havana, and so she went off with a trumpet player to New Orleans. He followed after her and talked her into coming to Cubop City and moving in with him, making many promises they both knew he'd never keep. She was sensational and danced her way through all the clubs in the city. Divórciate, mi negro, she would say to him. It is me you love. She was right. Chano loved Cacha, but he didn't trust himself. He loved a lot of women. He fell asleep thinking of her.

It was close to seven o'clock when he woke, and the apartment was in deep shadow. He lit a cigarette and lay back in bed, flicking the ashes on the floor. Cacha wouldn't be home before he left and that unsettled him. Everybody's busy in this town, everybody's after one thing or another. He hoped for a good audience; snow never kept people away, or the cold. This was Cubop City, just like Havana, except bigger and richer. Before leaving he rolled a joint, sat on the easy chair, and smoked it. Good stuff, not the crap El Cabito sold him last week. He saw the forest in all its clarity, every tree delineated, each leaf apart from every other leaf, each vine twirling around itself, each bush growing in its proper place, and all together a dense green mass: the smell of the air, the damp earth, the birds squawking overhead. There was no sign of the panther.

He was impervious to the cold and he walked up Lexington toward El Río, determined to find El Cabito. A block away he saw a lone figure under a streetlight. It was not a night for strolling. Maybe it was someone who couldn't stand to be in the house with his family. Winter will do that. He was dressed in green and yellow and was chewing on a chicken bone. Chano knew the sign: Orula, the oldest and wisest saint. When Chano was a few steps from him, the man stopped chewing and spoke: It's a hard night. He wore a scarf around his face that hid his features and gave him the look of a monk. There was an underlying hum, like that of a machine, coming from the vegetable world, where the santos lived. Chano was at the border of a dream, about to enter and be mounted again. He struggled with Changó, he couldn't let it happen now, and the saint got angry and abandoned him. The man's voice seemed to come from the sun, the dark inside the sun that only appears at night. Prepare yourself, he said.

For what? Chano thought. He smiled at the man, but inside he felt like a hen that couldn't lay an egg. He remembered the panther and how it had climbed on him at the restaurant and he had to shake it off. He ignored the warning and kept walking into the night. One hundred yards away he was a small figure amid the whiteness; two hundred yards away the forest shut behind him. What you create is yours. Drunk on palm wine, Obatalá, the saint of the north, made twisted children.

Chano saw the red neon light spilling onto the snow before he saw the place. He wanted to get some satisfaction from Cabito, then go to his gig. Without honor there's no music and the drums sound dead; without honor you might as well be like a million other fools shitting their pants from the cold. Chano looked through the window into the Río. El Cabito was sitting at a corner table with two other men, drinking beer and eating croquetas. Having a good time, laughing a lot.

Chano entered and headed straight for their table, unsmiling. He wanted to settle the matter so he could play his drums. It was that simple.

Cabrón, he said to El Cabito. You sold me chicken-shit and I want my money back.

Still sitting, El Cabito smiled and said, What I sell is what I sell and no one complains. Ask your girlfriend about that.

What did you say? Chano said. There was nothing he could see but that mocking smile, the gold tooth glinting with the overhead light of El Río.

She's had my stuff. Ask her.

The two men he was sitting with moved away. They saw the forest close in around Chano and El Cabito. Only one of them was coming out.

Chano pushed aside the table and went for him, throwing a wild punch that grazed his shoulder, then a straight right to the head that caught El Cabito on the cheek and threw him against the wall. El Cabito was stocky but quick. In one motion he ducked to avoid Chano's left hook and pulled a gun from his belt.

When the first bullet hit him, Chano felt as if he'd walked into a brick wall. He tried to force his way through it and take another swing at El Cabito. His arm flailed and dropped to his side. He looked down at his chest but couldn't see where the bullet entered him. Then he heard two more shots and felt them thumping into him. His legs weakened and he couldn't get enough air in his lungs. All sounds in the restaurant stopped. He wanted to see beyond the forest, go back home and lie down, but he had no strength left, and so he sat down on a chair, just to rest a little, get his breath back. The next shot hit his heart. Chano's head slumped and he dropped to the floor, where El Cabito put three more bullets into him. After that all you could hear was Changó's laughter coming out of the forest.

Sixty blocks away in midtown, Cacha was sniffing a sample of perfume on her inner wrist and chatting by the counter with two friends about men and their ways, how much like

193

boys they are, how they sometimes try to fool others but are only fooling themselves. Like Chano, Cacha said. He doesn't realize it but that man is in my hands. Ese negro tá pa mi. She grew quiet a moment and turned inward, her forehead clouding over with dark thoughts. What if he isn't? What if he goes back to his wife? Then she heard something like Chano's drumming, and the cloud passed as clouds do. She'd get him to divorce that woman in Cuba; she'd get him to marry her and live in the proper way in a big apartment with rose-colored walls and silk brocade curtains, he with his music, she with her children, drinking the milk of Ochún. She turned to one of her friends and said she felt warm inside. No matter how cold it was outside, she was always feeling warm.

NATIVITY

Bleating like a purple bloody lamb, afflicted with all that air and sound and smell, all those new creatures, all the to-do of nurses and doctors around him, Angel crossed the Rubicon that divides nonbeing from being. *Puer iactus est.* He was swaddled in blue sheets and a heavy cotton blanket, then nestled on the crook of his mother's arm, and from that position he discovered an enormous fleshy fruit with a chewy center. He immediately took it in his mouth and bit into it with his gums until it released the intoxicating juice that settled and satisfied him. During this time he forgot all other aspects of the new, multifarious world into which he'd been cast and concentrated not on the taste (what did he know about taste?) but on the quantity of fluid filling his mouth and belly and dribbling out the edges of his lips. All the while he was surrounded by the tones of teary moans coming from his mother and, a few minutes later, the laughter of his father, who was allowed to enter the room in order to observe what he had made by a simple, spasmodic release of sperm.

Is he all there? he asked, turning to Dr. Abreu, the high priest of the birthing altar. Angel's father meant, no doubt, to ascertain that the boy was a fully formed male.

The doctor, who had heard the question from anxious fathers a myriad times, had gained a reputation for his competence and was in high demand in the city among middle-class mothers with social ambitions. It was no small matter of pride to answer, when asked, that Dr. Abreu had delivered the child at the Centro Médico, where ladies of the highest estate went to have their babies. Consequently, he was becoming immensely rich as he populated the ranks of the classes who could afford him. He was, however, bored by his profession, which he considered not much more than midwifery with an advanced degree, and by his beautiful wife, a former nightclub dancer who was as frigid as a cod in winter, at least toward him. All of Havana knew that he'd much rather be big-game hunting in Africa with his good friend Hemingway or deflowering Indian maidens in the deepest parts of the Darien with his other good friend Graham Greene.

He will lead a good life, the doctor said, pulling off his surgical gown.

Had anything been seriously wrong, the boy's father would have been immediately consulted about what measures to take. For, the good doctor's success was not just due to his medical talents and his Harvard education, but to his willingness to consider solving the complications of birth in the most discreet and expeditious form possible at quadruple his normal fee, especially if he was in the midst of planning a trip.

To the doctor's question, Do you want him circumcised? his father could only mumble an incomprehensible answer, which the hunter doctor must have taken as a sign of severe parental distress, and so he did what he would have done had the boy been his own and left him with prepuce immaculate, a decision for which Angel would remain grateful for the rest of his life.

Angel's birth was a great moment in the history of his family: firstborn of the firstborn. Celebrations planned and dominated by his paternal grandmother lasted for days to the chagrin of his parents, who would have preferred to celebrate by themselves in the cocoonlike serenity of parental bliss. On the first day came forty-five members of the immediate family, who drank, sang, and danced until dawn of the following morning. On the second day were added close friends and lost relatives and a five-piece charanga band hired by Angel's uncle. On the third and fourth day, as news spread around the neighborhood and beyond, strangers showed up, among them three off-duty policemen, two kleptomaniacs, who stole a number of his grandmother's tchotchkes, and an ambulating chiropodist, who offered his services free of charge to any woman under thirty. On the last day, when Angel's grandmother lay in bed exhausted and all the other relatives had long gone to their homes to rest their vocal chords, their feet, and their livers, a coal seller with his face and hands smudged black from his labor sat on the porch eating leftover pork and drinking the last of the rum, and a woman in a black dress, believed to be the amiguita of the charanga's trumpet player, leaned against the trunk of the poinciana in the backyard, weeping copiously for no apparent reason. A dark portent? No, his grandmother said as she spied the woman from her bedroom window. A simple accident of fate. She directed that Eulipio, the neighborhood taxi driver, should be hired to take the woman where she wanted to go, and she declared the celebration over. Coño, Angel's father said when he heard her pronouncement. Praised be God!

THE PALACE
OF CRYSTAL

In one of Amanda's stories, titled "The Palace of Crystal," a teenage boy having lunch at a diner overhears a conversation between a man and a woman seated in the booth behind him. They are discussing the nature of tenderness. The boy assumes the man is older from the way his voice strains at the end of each statement. The man believes that tenderness is insecurity disguised as physical generosity. Love me tender. The woman, who is upset by the man's comment, tries to disagree with him. She is on the edge of anger, but her response is controlled. *Love me tender* means to love with something other than the lust in your mind. There is no love without lust. The boy is eating a hamburger and french fries, and he sides with the man, though he doesn't fully understand what the disagreement is about. It appears that the man and woman have had this conversation before.

It's a biological matter. Darwinism at work.

The boy, who is still a virgin, thinks about sex constantly. He would like to see what the woman looks like, but he doesn't want to give himself away by turning around. He imagines her with black curly hair and dark eyes, slim but shapely with round firm breasts.

What does *tender* mean anyway?

To offer, the woman says.

To hold, the man says. Greed, that's what it is, disguised as affection.

The boy wonders what they're eating, whether they had sex this morning, whether she screams or moans or whimpers. It's a slow day, a Friday without school and his parents at work. His friends? He hasn't any.

The story then shifts to the man and woman. They're not married, though the man would like to be. The woman is not sure. He is twenty years older and not eager to have children. He likes sex, often and constant and lustful. She is twenty-eight and has waited patiently for the right man. As if the age difference is not enough, he is Catholic—educated by Jesuits, no less—and Cuban, two markers that will not sit well with her family, who are secular but nonetheless committed Jews. At times he gets rough and says things that offend her. If there is tenderness in him, it is hidden under the sloppy, groaning venality she recoils from. Still, she is in love with him, or has convinced herself she is, and so she hesitates to end the relationship. If courage is abandon, she is a coward. So is he, but for different reasons. What if she misses this opportunity and no other comes along?

And so she engages in the discussion, hoping to find some common ground at last, a little sliver of an intellectual sandbank on which the two might stand as the waters of life rush past. That will be enough, no? Then on to other differences, which multiply daily.

The relationship between the man and the woman at the diner is not rigidly structured. It is constantly in motion, mutating, growing, and diminishing. It can be extinguished, it can cease to exist, and the man and the woman who fed it will walk away from each other. After some time, a month, a year, or five, their time together will be a mere wisp of a memory, a frisson, an embarrassment even, without the fixity or permanence of geometry.

And who is this boy? Why should he care about these two people, arguing over words? He would give anything to be with a woman. He doesn't care the least about love, its complications, its convolutions, how it tethers you to illusion, how it liberates you from the dull accumulation of time, the day off, the greasy hamburger, the lack of friends. He finishes his lunch, pays the bill, and goes outside. A cold wind hits him in the face and he walks down the empty main street of the small New Jersey town where he lives. He is wearing a T-shirt, a light jacket, and no hat and he enters a newly opened book and gift shop. The store is empty except for the attendant, a blonde college-age girl, who smiles kindly at him and goes back to scribbling in a notebook. The boy browses the shelves, mostly self-help books. There will come a time when he will read a dozen of these seeking ways of coping with his unhappiness, but now they seem miserable, pathetic texts. To the side, on the wall perpendicular to the bookshelves, is a glass shelf with New Age talismans—dream catchers, prisms, rocks of different shapes, small silver unicorns, and several crystals that catch the light from the track lighting on the ceiling and reflect it back at the boy. Illuminated, he remembers days when the sea shone back at him like that.

Can I help you? asks the girl. She has walked over and is standing next to him.

Na, says the boy. Just looking.

It's cold out today, she says.

He nods and says yeah under his breath. Real cold.

You're not dressed for it, she says.

I thought it'd be warmer. He is looking beyond her at the cars on the street, trying to avoid her eyes.

What's your name? she asks in a friendly enough way.

The boy hesitates. He's not sure what name to give her. Tadeo, he says. They call me Tad at school.

He begins to get an erection, which he tries to hide by bending slightly at the waist.

What shall I call you? asks the girl, who's noticed Tadeo's strange posture.

I hate to be called Tad, he says.

Okay, Ta-de-o, she says and walks back to the counter.

He turns his back to her and concentrates on the objects on the shelves. He waits until the erection subsides, then goes to the counter where she is sitting, pen in hand, notebook before her.

What's your name? he asks.

Amanda is my given name. My mother calls me Eye-fur.

Eye-fur?

Yeah. She claims I have an eye for everything. She laughs heartily.

Oh, he says, rocking back and forth on the balls of his feet, feeling like a tree about to crash in the forest; then, rummaging deep into himself—his shyness is excruciating—he finds enough courage to ask what she's writing.

I'm writing a story, she says.

What about?

People. What they do and why. For example, I just wrote that a boy entered the store and you did.

Oh, he says. He can't tell if she is kidding or if she really is some sort of clairvoyant. He looks down at the glass case, which houses some silver jewelry, opals, and many types of crystals. Are you in school?

I graduated college this past January. I'm trying to save up for graduate school. What about you?

There is no way a college graduate will have anything to do with him, and he is tempted to lie but decides against it. I'm a junior at the high school.

No school today?

No. Teacher-training day.

You have an unusual name, Tadeo.

It's Spanish for Thaddeus. I was born in Cuba.

You're the second Cuban I know.

I'm the only one I know.

And your parents?

They're Polish, but they're still in Cuba. I have American foster parents.

At this point the door jingles and a middle-aged man walks in. Amanda greets him effusively and plants a furtive kiss on his lips, which makes the man stiffen noticeably. From his voice Tadeo identifies him as the man from the diner. He senses more than a friendly relationship between the two, and he is right. Not long ago they were lovers. There remains a strong attraction between them, and they speak in the code of love, or former love, a wisp of smoke escaping from the embers. This is what Tadeo intuits, in their words, their body language, the way they move in relation to each other in a dance only they know the steps to. The man, it turns out, is Amanda's former college teacher. Their affair began when their eyes locked in an elevator, then through several classes until they moved in together—what else was there to do?—and lived in a cabin on the hill, surrounded by tall grass and wildflowers. In his imagination. The reality was something else. Quite romantic, to tell the truth, but all romance begins to sallow; all passion fallows. The fire on the lake dies down. The oily water once fed tall flames that lit the forest and the meadows. Now it is stagnant. The lake was a sea stretching beyond the horizon. Myopic to consequences, they couldn't see an end to their love. Amanda fought indifference as much as she could. She loved the man, admired him, but in the end the cabin became a prison and she went away.

The man suffered. Every piece of furniture, every floorboard spoke of her absence. Grief can envelop and encrust the writer's imagination, and it did the man's for a long time. To this day he is unable to write. He still lives in the cabin, now with the woman he was with in the diner.

Tadeo is about to leave the store, but then he hears Amanda introducing him to the man. This, she says, is Tadeo. He is Cuban, too.

What is a Cuban doing in this godforsaken town? the man asks.

Tadeo doesn't know how to answer the question. He's here because he's not anywhere else. This is where I was sent.

Do you like it? the man asks. His voice sounds winded, defeated.

It's okay, I guess.

Where do you live?

With the Aldersons, answers Tadeo, uncomfortable with the interrogation. He's not interested in finding out about this man's life and wishes he would go away. Then he could have Amanda to himself.

The Aldersons are good solid citizens of the town, at least they appear that way. The truth is that Mr. Alderson is a cross-dresser, and he likes to parade around the house in women's clothes when no one's around. Tadeo saw him once when he got home early from school, and he was so embarrassed that he went to his room and wouldn't come out for three days. At the end of the third day, Mr. and Mrs. Alderson sat him down in the living room and explained that he shouldn't judge Mr. Alderson unfairly. Cross-dressing is a perfectly normal activity, Mrs. Alderson said. Many people do it, and it doesn't mean that Mr. Alderson is a homosexual. Tadeo remained unconvinced.

Amanda's story is becoming more complicated than she wants. Her marginal notes indicate that she has to integrate the man into the story. She should have left him out from the beginning. She's written that Tadeo and the man are both from Cuba. Now she will be forced to have them interact, and she doesn't know the least bit about being Cuban, except for black beans and rice. What will they say to each other? Will they speak in Spanish? She's seen Spanish speakers use their hands when speaking but never with Americans present. She was hoping to be done with the story; then she could go on to something different, but she can't yet. So, they are Cuban. The man will ask Tadeo where in Cuba he is from. Havana—she knows no other Cuban cities, though it would be easy enough for her to check a map, do a search on the Internet. The rest of Cuba is a blur to her.

What part? the man wants to know: a further complication. So, she will have to go to the Internet after all and find a suitable neighborhood where Tadeo's parents might reside. Once that is solved they will go on to talk about the parents. His father is an engineer. He and Tadeo's mother left Poland for Cuba in 1970 to help build a power plant. They liked it so much they stayed. Tadeo, reticent by nature, provides the merest amount of information. In parting, the man gives Tadeo his phone number. Make sure you call me. We'll have you over for dinner. Amanda feels left out, but she can't very well invite herself. The man is living with that other woman, the woman in the diner, who doesn't believe in lust. The man pecks Amanda on the cheek, shakes Tadeo's hand, and leaves. There, Amanda writes. Case closed.

Will you teach me about Cuba? she asks Tadeo.

What do you want to know?

What your neighborhood was like, what you did for fun, that sort of thing.

We lived in an old house that was divided into apartments.

Do you miss your parents?

My father's sick. He's got pleurisy. We played chess together. My mother takes care of him.

Is it a nice apartment?

No. It's falling apart. All of Havana is falling apart. Not like here. Here the houses are in good shape. They're fixed up. The power never goes out. The plumbing works. My parents will never come to this country. My father says he wants to die in Poland. My mother laughs at him. She says Poland is too cold. Do you live with your mother? he asks, feeling a slight flicker of confidence.

She lives in California. I live by myself, in an apartment. As she writes, Amanda feels increasingly attracted to the boy. She's never known anyone so awkward, as if he were blind and had never learned facial expressions. He cannot keep from cracking his knuckles when he talks or moving his arms in random patterns. He is sincere and needy, and loneliness seems to ooze out of him. She wants him to be smart, a chess prodigy, perhaps, but he's not the type. Besides, she's sure she'd find a chess prodigy boring.

What's your apartment like?

It's okay, it's very small. It's okay. Would you like to see it?

Yes, he says so softly it is barely audible.

I get off at seven tonight. It's only two blocks away.

There's a break in the story here, and scribbled in the margins are notes about finding a way of transitioning from the scene at the store to the apartment, and from there to her bed, for that is where she wants to take Tadeo, make love to him, rid him of some of the neediness. Maybe he'll meet her at the store at seven and they will walk together. Maybe he'll show up at the apartment door with a bottle of wine. What does a teenager know about wine, and where would he get it? No. Everything between now and the bed scene is irrelevant. After the note, the story simply jumps.

Tadeo is awkward in bed but not so awkward that he doesn't kiss her softly, then more ardently, biting her lower lip and playing with her tongue. He comes in a quick shudder followed by a thrust that reaches the deepest parts of her. After a few minutes he wants to do it again, and that's when Amanda realizes that she's breaking the law. He's only fourteen. Lying in bed next to him, she thinks perhaps she should go back into the story and make him older, legalize him, and avoid another complication that would take several pages to straighten out, then decides to hell with it. She likes him as he is. He's a virgin and she's deflowering him. It wouldn't take much for her to love this boy much as she might love a pet or a favorite plant. She can watch him grow, turn into something, go off somewhere where he might become a chess champion or a car salesman.

The man who entered the store will stay in the small town teaching at the local college and looking out over the sea of his imagination, which increasingly becomes subordinate to his memory. Close to sixty, he wants comfort above all else, though it fails him often enough. Inside he feels no older than Thaddeus, waiting for someone to tell him that he has permission to lead the life he leads—a nice man who beds down women decades younger and sends them off wiser and stronger. He will grow older, perhaps with that dark-haired woman with whom he argues constantly, but more likely alone, his belly growing softer, his mind less able to leap playfully over the grave, waiting for fate to give him what he's due. Chances are he will die away from the land of his birth. For all his protestations to the contrary, his habits are thoroughly North American. Beans give him gas, and flan raises his blood sugar to alarming levels. He stumbles when speaking Spanish and avoids places where Cubans might congregate. Great changes don't come to a sixty-year-old man.

What about Amanda? She will suffer solitude in this small town, but she is young enough to pursue her talents. Tragedy will come in small, manageable doses. She will go to graduate school, publish many stories, have five children by different men, and live the rest of her life in the west, tending gladiolas, raising finches and songbirds, hundreds of them, that will turn her house into a palace of music.

DROWNING IN
A GLASS OF WATER

Years later as the crow flies, it occurred to Angel on the spur of the moment to call Amanda. He'd been driving up the California coast, and, via an Internet search that cost him $29.95, he found her in a small town south of San Jose. He had a double bourbon for courage at a bar at the edge of town and dialed her number. Naturally there was surprise in her voice as he identified himself, but she followed her greeting with the question What kept you so long? Things, time, vectors, he answered. You married? he asked. Yes, she said, with two sons. And you? she asked. He took a drink before answering, Not now, then asked about her husband, what he did. Works on a oil rig in Alaska. How romantic, he said, trying for humor. It came out like a barb. Who said marriage was romantic? she said. Where are you calling from? A bar. It's called Quigley's. I know it. I'm there, she said. And your kids, he wanted to say, but she'd already hung up.

The truth was that he was suddenly afraid what life had done to her in the intervening years and told himself he wasn't ready to see her, briefly considering paying the bill and leaving. Instead, he ordered another drink and sat back on the stool, taking in the oceanfront establishment, where the scents of stale beer, sea, and cleaning fluid mixed uncertainly in the dead hours between lunch and dinner. Upscale Irish bar in California. How far west can you go before you stop being Irish? How far north before you stop being Cuban? He remembers eating in a Japanese restaurant in Madrid where the sushi tasted like criadillas, bull testicles. Go east far enough, fast enough, and you wind up in eighteenth-century Kyoto writing haiku to the emperor.

Several drinks later Amanda appeared on the stool next to him. Hi, she said, and made no excuse for being two hours late. He forced his eyes to focus, offered a faint smile—she was, after all, late beyond all measure of decorum, and she knew he hated waiting, unless the waiting was self-imposed. He was about to ask her what she wanted when the bartender placed a drink before her, vodka on the rocks with a dozen olives. You a regular? he asked. Sort of, she said. I work here two days a week. What happened to your insouciance? he asked, trying to keep his Cuban accent in check and failing. It invariably surfaced after more than two drinks, shortening the vowels, clipping some of the final syllables.

It's alive and well, she said with that tart western voice of hers, or was it her confidence—he'd never known anyone so full of confidence—or was it her eyes that fixed on him until all his defenses crumbled into lumps of brick dust? I have two boys to support. She had a husband working in Alaska, making, he was sure, a healthy amount of money. Support was a euphemism for something else. Boredom?

There was a lull in the conversation. He ordered another drink, though he was well beyond his limit. You were very late, he said rewinding the film to the beginning, a way of filling the silence between them. She responded that she was setting the boys up; she had the rest of the afternoon free, and hearing this he felt a chill run up his spine. He had wanted to see Amanda very badly when he'd first called. Now he thought calling might have been a mistake. She had a life worlds away from what they'd had or he thought they had—the cottage on the hill, the tall grass, the big sky, the fantasy that grew from his heart, his penis, until reality could not compete. You are happy, he said. It was a statement for which he was seeking assent. I have good days, I have bad days, she said. Are you drunk? I'm alone, he said. You are, she said. You're drunk. He leaned back on the chair, wanting to disengage, go away, fly back home. His life had become puny, peripheral; hers central, indispensable. Amanda called the bartender over and ordered food. They know what I like. That must be comforting, he said. And dull, she said. Small town. Everyone knows you. Children, he said. They'll do that to you.

In forty-eight hours he'd be in Cubop City, out of the flickering past and back in the present, where all things happen. He dreaded it. For now, he had Amanda before him. At thirty a woman doesn't yet show her age, and Amanda looked as good as she did at twenty. He found himself desiring her, though it seemed ludicrous considering how far and long they'd drifted from each other. At one point she leaned her head on his shoulder and his hand drifted to her thigh and stroked it. She let him, and he fell back into a miserable nostalgia. She, he, the hill overlooking the ocean, the late-afternoon sun, a song playing on the old radio they kept in the kitchen. Then back to the din of the bar, getting crowded with the happy-hour crowd, and Amanda off to another life, a Paul Bunyan husband, suburban boys who played soccer. She was the same; she was completely different, leading the life of American dreams, and yet, magically disengaged from that life, as if she had allowed herself this little slice of paradise and was simultaneously aware that at any time she would be swallowed by the maw of Saturn or some other divine glutton. That's what made her irresistible—how she was the embodiment of grace before despair. He didn't feel love for her at that moment. He felt marvel.

STORYTELLER

Stories were not cures. The cancer was final. Papa knew that and—truth be told—was glad of it. Mama dead ten days and festering. He'd be dead soon enough and I'd be freed from having to come up every day with a fresh one, caught right off the river of my imagination, which was fervent enough, considering all the time and solitude, my survival amid the corrosion, the move to Cubop City. I wanted to be not just blind but invisible, inhabiting the page. I thought the world was contained in books, not books in the world. Then filial duty: to obey first, to defer second, to oblige third. Love as practice, not emotion, unquestioned, unchallenged, as genetic mandate in defiance of time and the oblique tendencies of self. Love as a crab. The word for claw in Spanish, tenaza, like love—tenacious. Real love, of the sort I couldn't help but practice: tenacious and therefore oppressive. Love did not contain the world. The world contained it and the world beat outside the door.

The work of storytelling: to stand on the banks of the river, fishing pole in hand, jerking at its merest tug and coming up empty, slackening the line so that the hook could drift to the deeper parts at the center where the water rippled with currents and countercurrents. Somewhere in those waters was the big fish that had avoided being caught, that would make all the waiting, the dreaming, worthwhile. I tried to envision it: white, allegorical, and massive. I'd have to use all my strength and cunning to reel it in, pull it up on shore, then hoist it over my shoulder for the long trek to the place where love resides and carries on. Every day I offered my parents whatever I'd managed to catch, aware that the big fish had eluded me. No cure.

They complained. Sometimes the fish was too long, sometimes it was too short. Sometimes it had a weird shape with pieces going in several directions at once so that it looked more like an octopus than a fish. Sometimes it croaked like a toad or hissed like a snake or chirped like a bird. Once I brought one so heavy and motionless it was like a chunk of vulcanized rubber; another time I caught a feather that hovered over the bed a moment, then floated off behind the dresser. My parents' silence, when they were silent, I took for assent. On rare occasions I might have heard a reluctant laugh or a grunt or a woeful sigh, but it was their silence I preferred, the story doing its proper work under the surface, through their veins, and into their organs, what was left of them.

Papa looked up from the bed with a smile, Mama dead and rotting beside him. Oh, the smell. The fish you bring us, he said, come from the depths. They suffer the maladies of creatures who have never known the sun. How about a surface fish awash in light?

How could I know surface when I didn't know light? I kept that question from Papa. He would call me obfuscator, sophist, tautologist—words that wounded me not. I was already scar, regret, compunction, guilt. Rent by emotions, I quivered like a reed in shallow water.

SWIMMING TO MIAMI

Out of gas and taking water where the prow had rammed into a piece of flotsam, the *Ana María* floated helplessly past the tall buildings of Miami, carried north by the Gulf Stream at great speed. When Johnny Luna realized that they might miss their destination altogether and wind up circling the Sargasso Sea forever, he took to the oars and began rowing as hard as he could toward the shore. Obdulio, his mind too simple or too complex to understand the situation, sat on the leather Chrysler seat and stared at the high clouds morphing into a myriad of shapes over the Florida Peninsula.

He saw a panther biting the neck of a lion, a ballerina leaping over a bishop, a giraffe on fire, ten angels pissing into a bottle, an old man with a crooked nose and a single horn growing from his forehead, a beast with the head of a crocodile and the wings of a bat, a baseball player who had just struck out, an ox, a 1956 Buick, and a pregnant mare with the face of the Virgin Mary.

¡Coño! We're going by Miami, Johnny said, interrupting Obdulio's catalog.

After two hours his hands were raw and bleeding, his upper back felt like someone had taken a baseball bat to it, and his arms were as heavy as concrete. Obdulio woke from his catalog and pointed out a stretch of shore toward which they could aim. In a final burst of energy Johnny rowed the last two hundred yards like a galley slave until the *Ana María* nosed itself onto the sand. Johnny jumped off the boat to secure it, and as he did so, a group of naked men and women came running to help. Johnny couldn't believe what he was seeing.

¡El Paraíso! Obdulio screamed as he took off his shirt.

Paraíso no, an old man in the group said. Haulover Beach.

He was wiry and brown and his long hair was tied in a ponytail. He was surrounded by equally tanned people, all of them naked except for a few wearing straw hats and old baseball caps. By now the group of nudists had pulled the *Ana María* off the water and were walking around it admiring its construction.

Miami? Johnny asked. Obdulio had taken off his clothes and was dancing around the group, who were as happy to see him naked as he was to see them. ¡Eto tá buenísimo, buenísimo! Obdulio said as he was embraced by a lanky and very jolly woman whose breasts flapped against his face.

Miami down there, the old man said, pointing to the south. About five miles. Welcome to America!

Johnny gave a pained smile. He never liked being unclothed in front of others, just as he never liked others unclothed in front of him, not even his wife. Now his emotions were experiencing a strange reversal, and he felt a growing discomfort at having his clothes on in front of the nudists. Modesty got the best of him, however, and all he could do was take off his shirt, which he folded neatly, though it was smudged and wrinkled and smelled of gasoline, and placed on top of a plastic cooler. His shoes he had left behind on the boat, wrapped in plastic so they wouldn't get wet.

The nudists led Johnny and Obdulio to their encampment about fifty yards away, and soon they were sitting on the sand devouring ham sandwiches and drinking beer. Johnny's embarrassment was gone along with his shirt. He looked over at the *Ana María,* glistening in the sun, and was overcome with emotion. He'd failed to cross six times, and he made sure he wouldn't fail again by building a solid, beautiful boat. Except for the piece of sea junk that had opened a breach in the starboard side of the prow, the *Ana María* had held and taken them safely across. There wasn't a better boat anywhere. With tears in his eyes, he raised his fifth bottle of Mexican beer and said in his best American-movie English, I want to be thanking you very much. Viva los Estados Unidos, Viva la libertad! Obdulio followed suit, and so did the rest of the nudists, except for a fellow with a handlebar mustache who looked like an overweight Jerry Colonna. He complained about aliens taking over the country.

You can't go anywhere without running into these people, even Europe, he said, chewing on a piece of carrot smeared with onion dip that stuck to his mustache.

A middle-aged woman with the breasts of a seventeen-year-old girl said, In this country you're free to do as you wish, and as far as I'm concerned everyone is welcome, especially the hungry and the oppressed. She looked over at Obdulio, her face bathed in compassion.

I don't know about oppressed, the man with the mustache said, but these boys look pretty well fed to me.

Johnny had had his fill of food and drink and wanted to move on. He was seeing double and the beach was tilting away from the ocean. Obdulio was still eating. His cheeks were smeared with mayonnaise, and it looked to Johnny like he was getting an erection, though he wasn't sure. It might have been the way Obdulio was sitting.

He was about to order him to get his clothes on when they heard voices in the distance and turned to see a man in a gray suit and a woman in high heels followed by a cameraman. The three were tramping in their direction, past an animated volleyball game and a European family that seemed never to have lost paradise, let alone regained it.

Obdulio, Johnny said, ponte la ropa. Obdulio started fumbling for his clothes, but it was too late. With his mouth full of ham, lettuce, and whole-wheat bread, he mumbled something back and smiled. Bits of ham were stuck in between his teeth and he looked like a shark that had swallowed a pig whole.

Not to worry, said the old man with the long hair. Es el television his-pánico.

Yes, me worry, said Johnny. He quickly retrieved his shirt and put it on.

Where are the balseros? asked the male reporter. He was a tall, handsome Cuban American with a voice trained to be deep and professional. He was out of breath, and sweat dribbled down the sides of his face. From the looks of it he had pulled this kind of duty before—balsero stories were a dime a dozen in those days—and he was not too happy; nor was the woman, who kept rearranging her hair and smacking her lips. She had to balance her considerable girth on Manolo Blahnik shoes, which sank all the way into the sand every time she moved. She complained about the heat and her puñetero producer, who kept giving her shitty assignments.

If it were up to me, said the cameraman, they would all sink in the sea. Que se ahoguen pal carajo.

Johnny and Obdulio stood up. Johnny tucked his shirt into his pants. Obdulio was still naked, his penis at half mast.

The female reporter shook her head dejectedly and looked away. The cameraman fidgeted with his camera. The male reporter, holding the microphone to his mouth as if the taping had already begun, wanted to know what had happened to the raft.

The *Ana María* no is a raft, Johnny said. He pointed at the boat. I built it I myself.

We were told there was a raft, said the reporter. You could cross the Pacific on a boat like that.

I work on it six months each night, Johnny said in proud deliberate English. He tried to sound like Ricardo Montalbán in *Fantasy Island*.

Martínez, the male reporter called out to the cameraman. Why don't you break the boat up a little. Make it seem more weather beaten, ¿tú sabes?

Martínez gathered up some dry seaweed and placed the camera carefully on it, making sure it didn't touch the sand. Then he started throwing karate kicks at the prow of the *Ana María*.

Johnny felt like his very grandmother was being kicked to death.

¡Coño! Johnny said. What are you doing? Then he jumped on Martínez, who fell backward and scurried away on his hands and feet like a crab, kicking up sand as he went.

El tipo está loco, man, the cameraman said. He stood and looked over at the camera. The male reporter held Johnny back.

It is my boat, Johnny said.

Take it easy, the male reporter said.

When things had settled down and Martínez was a safe distance away, the reporter explained to Johnny that crossing the Straits of Florida was a dangerous thing, and lots of people had lost their lives trying. Johnny said that that was because they didn't know what they were doing. The reporter said he understood, but they couldn't run a story on television about someone who had made the crossing on a sturdy boat he built himself. You are either trying to flee communism or off on a pleasure cruise, and believe me, nobody's interested in two guys on a pleasure cruise. This boat looks brand-new. Now he was lecturing the group of nudists around them. We need to show how hard it is for the people, how much they are having to sacrifice, even their own lives, in order to escape the tyranny of Castro.

He stopped, wiped his brow with a silk handkerchief he pulled from the front pocket of his jacket, and added as an afterthought, Too bad we don't have a mandarria.

What's a mandarria? one of the nudists asked.

A sledgehammer.

That's all Johnny needed to hear.

Me cago en el coño de tu madre, he said to the reporter. On that note he sounded like nobody but himself. You underestan, idiota? ¡Me cago en el recontracoño de tu madre!

He grabbed the microphone from the reporter's hand and threw it into the sea.

That's a five-hundred-dollar mike, the reporter said, running into the surf and trying to retrieve it. He came out dripping wet, his suit ruined, his pink silk tie turned a corrugated brown. He stood inches away from Johnny and said, You'll pay for this, balsero de mierda, and ordered his crew to get out of the goddamn beach. The female reporter had taken off her expensive shoes and her jacket and given up on her hair, letting the sea breeze blow gently through it. She didn't seem half-bad that way, more relaxed and easygoing. As she ambled toward the exit through the sand dunes, she turned and looked out over the water searching the horizon for God knows what: a sailboat, a respite, a good story.

The police found Johnny and Obdulio walking south toward Miami Beach on Route A1A. Obdulio was fully dressed and was even sporting a New York Yankees cap one of the nudists had given him as a good-luck charm. Johnny hadn't been able to find his shoes in the boat, and so he went barefoot, hopping whenever he stepped on a pebble or a burr but otherwise happy they were headed in the right direction. He was singing boleros and looking forward to the day when there would be a woman on the other side of his love songs.

The police surrounded them with three vehicles, as if they were bank robbers or child rapists. Six officers spilled out, five in uniform, one in a sports jacket who spoke in the raspy baritone of Broderick Crawford. Johnny couldn't understand a thing. He was lost in a sea of language no American movie or television show would help unravel. The sky turned dark, and peals of thunder rolled over them, followed by lightning flashes far inland over the Everglades.

Johnny was afraid. Broderick Crawford was a tough cop and a drunk as well. He tried to explain their situation, but all that came out was a jumble of words that sounded like a lost language from a remote part of the Amazon. Obdulio was smiling his usual fool's smile and stood at attention giving the officers a military salute. Johnny shook his head. One of the uniformed officers handcuffed them and said something about remaining silent—Johnny caught that—and then he led them to the back of the paddy wagon. Just then the rain came down in thick sheets that made everything blurred. Mala fortuna, mala fortuna. Obdulio's face was twisted by apprehension and his eyes were wide open. He looked to Johnny for reassurance but found none.

Changó, Changó, he yelled. Ampáranos.

Changó was offering no protection today. The van moved with a lurch, then did a U-turn, and headed back north away from Miami, the two cruisers in front and the wagon following them, lights flashing, sirens wailing. It was too much for Johnny, who, exhausted from the last ten years of his life, the desperation, the secret planning, the work of building the *Ana María,* and weary from the hangover that was beginning to manifest itself in every cell of his brain, began to blaspheme God with such ferocity that God himself—if there is one—must have trembled in his heavenly seat. It rained hard, harder than Johnny could curse and Obdulio could pray. And as suddenly as it started, the rain ceased and the sun came out again.

A few minutes later, when the water evaporated from the asphalt and the cars, turning the air into thick Florida soup, the caravan stopped. The van doors opened and Johnny and Obdulio were led into a glass and brick building and made to stand before a young officer sitting behind a tall desk. His head was clean shaven, and he said to them in rapid Miami Spanish that they were under arrest for vagrancy and recited their Miranda rights.

Vago, Johnny said. *Vago?* There were traces of Alfonso Bedoya's voice from *The Treasure of the Sierra Madre.* I'm no *vago.* I build my boat. Wood by wood. In Jaimanitas. Now we come to La Yuma to work more.

Johnny protested that he was a decent man. They'd landed among a group of nudists. It wasn't their fault.

¿Cómo? said the booking officer.

Era inevitable, Johnny said, lying slightly. They obligate us to take off our clothes. They say it is natural. In Ho-lo-beh Beach.

The booking officer turned to the two remaining arresting officers and translated for them what Johnny said. The three of them broke out in laughter, and Obdulio laughed, too, though he didn't understand anything. Only Johnny was serious, serious as stone, serious as someone who didn't want to get sent back to the hell he'd just left. While the officers figured out what to do, he sat on a bench directly across from the booking desk. Obdulio asked him what was going on and he said he didn't know.

The only thing I know is that I don't know anything, Johnny said, quoting a self-styled philosopher who lived in his neighborhood in Havana. Maybe they were dead and this is purgatory; maybe this is a way station on the way to paradise, or hell. He kept the thoughts to himself, not wanting to alarm Obdulio, who could go from elation to panic in an instant.

Someone brought Johnny a pair of sneakers that were too large for him, and they got back into the paddy wagon and drove to Haulover. They walked across the wide beach toward the nudists, to whom the policemen must have appeared like Nazi storm troopers—two big American men in black uniforms and a smaller Cuban American trailing behind, the two balseros hidden among them. The volleyball players stopped batting their ball and several of the nudists began to gather their things.

At the water's edge Johnny noticed that the *Ana María* had disappeared. He looked up and down the beach and back to the dunes that separated the road from the beach, even out to sea, thinking perhaps the tide had taken it. By this point the old man with the ponytail had come over to the troopers, and before he could speak to them, Johnny asked him in his frantic movie English where his boat was.

The Coast Guard sank it, the old man said.

What? Johnny said, though it came out sounding like *Guat*.

The Cuban American officer explained that that was what the Coast Guard did with all vessels that came illegally from Cuba. But Johnny should be happy. He had touched American soil. That meant he could stay. Wet foot, dry foot, remember that when you go before la migra. Wet foot, dry foot, he repeated slowly so Johnny could catch it.

Johnny didn't want to catch anything except a break. Crossing the Florida Straits had been his obsession for ten years. Now his obsession was gone along with the *Ana María*. He was here on solid ground. Wet foot, dry foot. He stood still a moment pondering whatever it was fate had prepared for him. He had set out for Miami and instead landed among a bunch of crazy nudists. ¡Qué cosa! Still in handcuffs, he started walking down the beach away from the group, increasing his gait as he heard the policemen's voices yelling to stop, and then he broke into a gallop, clopping along in his big sneakers until they slid from his feet and he could run freely. The voices got dimmer and finally stopped altogether. He felt like he had escaped demons wanting to pull him back, and just as he looked over his shoulder to see where they were, he tripped and landed with his cheek on the sand. For a moment he was stunned. He could see the waves moving up the beach and reaching his left arm; he could hear seagulls squawking overhead and the far-off hum of traffic. He could feel his breath as it moved in and out of his lungs and under that his heart beating loud and deep like a drum just before it breaks. He turned to face the sky. He'd never felt so tired. He closed his eyes a moment and heard Miami calling. He stood and wriggled his arms until the handcuffs slid from his wrists, then waded into the water, and swam toward her with long easy strokes. In his sleep he was swimming to Miami.

THE SPANISH
TINGE

Jelly Roll was with a woman when the Cuban showed up at his door looking for work. The Cuban was holding a horn case in his left hand. The right, long and graceful, dangled at his side and swung back and forth grazing against his pants.

At this hour? Jelly Roll asked. It's one o'clock. Good thing I'm done.

I'm not, the woman said.

Give me a minute, Jelly Roll said over his shoulder. Then he turned to the Cuban and asked his name.

The Cuban had not eaten very well in his life. His cheeks were hollow and his jacket hung loosely from his shoulders, pant cuffs barely below his ankles. He was wearing somebody else's suit.

Adalberto Fuentes, the Cuban said.

That's some name.

Yes, the Cuban said, looking beyond Jelly Roll to the woman. She was caramel colored with straight hair and full lips and she was very beautiful. The sheets were pulled all the way up to her neck.

A-dal-ber-to, the Cuban repeated. I need a job.

I'll call you Bert. Sugar, meet Bert, Jelly Roll said. He looked into the Cuban's eyes. Come by the club tomorrow at five. See if you can play that thing.

Adalberto turned on his heels and, in his elation, walked the three miles to Franklin Street, where all the Cubans stayed. There were flute players and piano players and bass men. Couple of violinists, half a dozen horn men. Adalberto acted like he was the only cornet player among them. He was cocky and ignorant, but he had a natural talent that was bigger than he knew how to handle. Two weeks in town and already he had an audition with Jelly Roll Morton.

Next day Adalberto was at the Toucan Cafe at 5 PM sharp. The place was closed, door locked. He lit a cigarette and waited. He looked right, then left. Children playing down the street, an old man on a horse-drawn cart clopping by, a couple of men lounging at the corner. It was humid hot and he could feel beads of sweat trickling down his back. He walked around to the back door, then returned to the front. By 6 PM he figured Jelly Roll had forgotten about him. That copper-colored lady ensnared him in her trap, Adalberto thought, and just as he was about to leave, a man in a white shirt and black bow tie came to the door and opened the place up.

You seen Jelly Roll? Adalberto asked in his best English.

What? the man said, scrunching his face.

Je-lly-Roll-Mor-ton.

He ain't here tonight. Jelly Roll never works Tuesday. Where you from?

Cu-ba, Adalberto said. I come here to play for Jelly Roll. He told me.

No Jelly Roll tonight, said the man, waving his hands sideways in front of his face. Or tomorrow. He's on the road to Chicago. Horns a dime a dozen in this town. Dime a dozen.

I can play for you.

The man gave a quick forced laugh like he'd just heard a bad joke.

I'm just a bartender, man. Tuesday's off night. You go ahead and play if you want. Keep me entertained while I set up. You better be good.

Adalberto wanted to say, Nobody's better than me, but he kept his mouth shut and played his cornet as if he were playing for Jelly Roll himself, and when he was done, the bartender repeated, Lots of good horns in this town. Nevertheless, he gave Adalberto the address of a club a few blocks away that might give him some work. Adalberto walked there and played again, his lips warm now, fingers loose, and the manager said he would try him out.

Ten dollars a week, plus a take of the door after one month. You don't show up the piano and you don't show up the bass player and you don't show up the clarinet. Otherwise, there's trouble and you're out of here in a whistle blow.

Adalberto did as he was told and became a sideman at the Palace Bar. Asked for nothing, lived like a rat in a falling-down excuse for a rooming house run by a deaf woman from Cienfuegos who didn't care the least about music, or cleanliness. Days he slept and lounged and ate; nights he spent at the Palace, getting thicker, deeper, broader in his playing, to the point where the other guys let him solo occasionally and he'd blare out sounds so hot big smiles opened in the crowd's faces, and they closed their eyes and moved to the music. Horn's supposed to lead. The bass had no choice but to follow along and the piano played the harmony. Afterward, Adalberto wasn't quite sure what had happened with the music but knew it was good.

One day in the middle of his solo he looked down at the audience and saw Jelly Roll Morton himself sitting at one of the front tables with a beautiful lady. Adalberto missed a note, which he thought no one noticed because it was in the middle of a riff that was going all over the place, and he made up for it by blowing so hard the wineglasses rattled, or seemed to, and the people winced and cupped their ears, wanting to hear and not hear at once. When the band was done with the set, the bass player suggested they go down and pay their respects to Jelly Roll. Adalberto turned him down saying if Jelly Roll wants to say hello, he can come to the bar.

What are you saying, boy? You don't treat Jelly Roll like that. He's the man.

Adalberto was still young, but he'd lost his innocence there in New Orleans—everybody did—and he'd more than made up for it with petulance. So while the other musicians hung around the famous man, Adalberto sat at the bar and ordered a beer and struck up a conversation with the bartender.

Lake Ponchartrain. He said that right. His English was a lot better now. Never seen a lake that big. Bartender said no. Have you seen a river as big as the Mississippi? Bartender said no. Have you ever heard a trumpet as good as mine? Bartender didn't answer.

I have, Adalberto heard a voice say behind him, and when he turned, he saw Jelly Roll, the beautiful lady hanging on his arm, the diamond on his front tooth gleaming with the light of the bar. The man loved his diamonds. You missed a note and tried to hide it with that riff. I know a horn player would have gone with that note to see where it led, then brought it back on a leash.

Who's that? What's his name?

Name don't matter. Always somebody better, Jelly Roll said. Then he kissed the lady on the jaw, right under the ear, turned her around, and left the room.

Jelly Roll was there the following night and the next, right on through the weekend. Never came back after that, however, and Adalberto was not to see him again for many years. Meanwhile he made the rounds of New Orleans clubs, got a girlfriend, lost her, got another, and left her because she wanted to get married. Music is my wife, he told her, feeling stupid and miserly afterward. He played with dozens of groups, doing parades and funerals, street competitions, most of which he won, except when he went up against Keppard and Emanuel Perez. Then he realized what Jelly Roll knew—there's always somebody better. He went back to Cuba to visit and was a big hit there, playing the swing with a little 6/8 measure and a blues syncopation he'd sneak in when he could, driving bandleaders crazy and audiences wild.

All kinds of things happening in New Orleans, he told his friends in Havana.

All kinds of things happening right here, his friends said.

You can't play the white clubs here, he said.

How about New Orleans?

White, tan, and black. Don't matter, long as you can play.

He told them about Buddy Bolden, best horn in the world. I heard he's gone crazy. Told them about Armstrong, a boy of fourteen, who was playing it up in the whorehouses of Storyville. Told them about Jelly Roll himself and what he'd done with piano rags. Then he had to explain what rags were: contradanza con chu-chu. Chattanooga choo-choo. Left hand striding, right hand keeping the melody.

His friends were impressed but not awed. They played with him and tried to outdo his innovations. Cuban music in those days was just coming out of danzón, mostly because people could dance to it slow and regal as if they were French nobility and not the white trash that had come from Spain or the free blacks that worked themselves out of the cane fields and wanted to be whiter than white. When the montuno part of the danzón came on, which is what the musicians really went for, the couples would stop while the ladies fanned themselves and the men talked nonsense with one another, waiting for the danceable parts to return.

The musicians listened. In the montuno was the mambo; in the montuno was the cha-cha-chá, although no one knew it at the time, and it occurred to them to stretch the montuno out until the dancers got tired of waiting for the slower movement and started dancing to the music, no matter that it was faster and more manic and made them sweat like they were in the jungle, el monte, leaping like lizards and mounting the women. That's where the word montuno comes from to begin with. Caballo, ¡qué te monte el santo! It was montuno they were after. The rest of the danzón was nineteenth century—the contredanse, the quadrille. That's not what Cuba was about.

Adalberto went back to New Orleans with what he'd learned, wanting to blow the winds of change through his lips. He began to play more brazenly, as if his life depended on it, and just like he'd amazed his friends in Cuba with the new American music, he amazed the New Orleans crowd with his montunos, playing in and out of ragtime, pushing through to something new no one had heard before, the habanera docking into port as it had done in Spain and France, where Bizet picked it up, and in Buenos Aires, where it blended with the milonga and became tango.

And then, when he was playing the kind of music that might make him famous and respected and, above all, rich, love struck. Love disguised as a soft dove, a kid glove. She was a beauty from Puerto Rico, a tiny brown-colored thing with slanted eyes and thin lips that betrayed some Oriental ancestry, and the loveliest swaying and grinding—when she wanted to grind—hips in the whole world. Meek and sharp with a brain like a sponge and a heart like a well.

All this came to him the first time he saw her, dancing with a Creole man in a tuxedo whose face was bloated with drink and drugs. Adalberto stopped his playing, no matter that he was in the middle of a riff somewhere between Havana and New Orleans, lowered his cornet, and started snapping the fingers of his right hand, keeping the beat like that, like that, his eyes fixed on her. The rest of the band put down their instruments and listened to his fingers snapping in clave, waiting to see what came next. Nothing did except Adalberto's stare, which the girl returned, ignoring the Creole man's bloodshot killer eyes. Adalberto wasn't even blinking—snap snap snap, snap snap—the audience barely breathing, the girl with the China eyes letting her mouth open into a sweet-and-sassy smile. The Creole man turned to her and had some words, took her off the dance floor, threw money on the table, and led her out. On his way he leaned over the manager, Little Red, who nodded officiously and gave a quick slicing look at Adalberto. Adalberto brought his cornet to his lips and resumed playing, the rest of the band did, too, and the crowd exploded. But something had changed. His playing had grown plaintive. Part of him was outside the club, chasing after the girl with the China eyes.

After the show, when the musicians were sitting at the bar, Little Red told Adalberto he was done at the club, paid him the twenty-five dollars he was owed, and said loud enough for the others to hear that he'd just made eyes at China, the girlfriend of one of the most powerful men in town.

Who's that man? Adalberto asked.

Bob Rowe, said the trombonist, the King of the Tenderloin. And that girl you were eyeing was his whore. Then the trombonist said to the manager that if Adalberto went, he went, too, a sentiment echoed by the bass player. Only the young clarinetist, who'd joined them a month before and had his own ambitions, remained silent.

Finding himself without a band, and not just a band, but the hottest young band in town, Little Red took back his words.

You back in, but you keep messing with his girls, you going to find yourself with a knife in your belly one of these days. Give me back the money.

That's my money, Adalberto said, pocketing the twenty-five. You owe it to me. No sin looking at a girl.

Every sin in the book in those eyes, Little Red said.

The clarinetist, who was barely seventeen, chuckled. Every sin in the book, he repeated. Every sin.

Adalberto went home feeling like there was a fly buzzing around him just beyond his reach. He spent a restless night, waking to China's eyes and her smile, then falling back asleep. It was too good to be a simple dream and not a portent.

The band played on a couple of weeks to the same upbeat crowds, and for that Little Red was grateful. Then Bob Rowe appeared again with the Puerto Rican girl and another wrapped around his other arm. After the set, Adalberto walked himself slowly over to Rowe's table and introduced himself to China, ignoring Rowe and the other girl. That was trouble, and when Little Red noticed—the man had eyes at the back of his head— he rushed to the table and ordered a bottle of champagne on the house. Rowe was not a strong or a particularly large man, but he had olive green eyes that went somewhere beyond hatred to the other side of the Milky Way. Voodoo eyes, they were called in those days. He'd killed men and he'd killed women. Adalberto sat at the table unasked and flirted with

China while Bob Rowe turned his champagne glass slowly and listened to the backup band, saying nothing to Adalberto until just before the second set, at which time he leaned over and whispered, I know just where it's going. Won't kill you, won't even make you bleed much, but every time you take a deep breath you gonna remember my name and how it was you stopped blowing so hard.

Bob Rowe never returned to the club. The musicians forgot about his words to Adalberto and continued to bring down the house every night. Already their reputation had spread beyond New Orleans, and there were a number of musicians, some envious, some just curious, coming to hear them play, especially the Cuban with the wild horn. Little Red finally got to relax a bit, but not so much that he didn't withhold their salaries as long as he could, not because he couldn't afford to pay them, but because that way he could keep them at the club instead of losing them to one of the fancier places uptown. They were young and more in need of adulation than money. They survived on tips, got free drinks at the bar after sessions, and had access to girls in Storyville at a discount when they needed them.

Early one New Year's Day, as Adalberto was walking home after dropping off a girl, someone came out of the shadows of predawn and stuck a knife into him all the way to the handle. On the ground, barely able to breathe, Adalberto felt his lung collapse. Right then he remembered Bob Rowe's words with such bitterness he could taste it coming out of his mouth and making little red bubbles on his lips. He wound up in the hospital cared for by the Ursuline sisters, who tried to convert him not with their words but with their soft caring ways, and there he waited until he could breathe right. After that he was never able to play his instrument again, not with the verve and heat that were his trademarks. He tried, God knows he tried, but forget the high notes and forget those long, slow ones he coaxed out of the horn. And when he realized it and when his band realized it and when the audience stopped listening and continued on with their drinking and their chatter, he walked away, simply and quietly.

Adalberto counts change in his room. Adalberto walks to the store for a can of beans, a loaf of bread, three cigarettes. His clothes, frayed, unwashed. He smells of kerosene and cheap wine, and his beard has turned different shades of gray.

A woman at the store suggests he take in students. He says he doesn't read music, never done any teaching. It's all ear. No money to get back to Cuba. Adalberto talks to himself, and the woman looks at him as if he were an apparition, not so strange a thing in New Orleans as people might think.

Next afternoon, the woman was at the door with her boy, eight years old or so, holding a case that was almost as big as he. Adalberto looked at the boy: dark skin, bow tie, brown jacket, pants bunching at his heels. Reminded him of himself at that age.

Where's your gig tonight? he asked the boy, who looked at him with scared Mississippi water eyes.

Dollar a lesson, the woman said.

That's fine, Adalberto said. Teach the boy a few tricks.

Adalberto might not have been able to read music, but he was a natural teacher. First he showed the boy how to blow without valves, just to get him used to the mouthpiece on the lips, then sent him home with some homework—fingering exercises, breath exercises, lip exercises, make them strong, keep them from cracking. Keep those lips moist, boy. Drink plenty of water. No milk. Phlegm gets in the way. Coffee's good but you're too young. Tea with honey's not bad.

By the end of that month he had two more students, and a month later he had three more. Six dollars a week. He could afford a bottle of whiskey now and then. Friends stopped by, men he'd played with, club managers. A couple of young horn players just starting out asked for lessons from the old master. Old master? Just for that he charged them double. They came sporadically when they were having difficulties playing. They drank with him, left tipsy. Don't ever play drunk. Mostly you get sloppy, then you get lazy. Musicians are lazy enough by nature. Never mentioned junk because it was below his dignity. That's how he taught, and the students looked up to him like someone sitting under a tree who's made friends with the wind. Not much wind in New Orleans unless a storm blows in.

In a year's time his reputation as a teacher had eclipsed his reputation as a musician. If you asked him, he'd answer he didn't know what music ought to be like. I just know what sounds good and what sounds bad and I try to turn the bad into the good. With some boys it's hopeless. I send them home and tell their parents he should learn another trade. That's what music is, a trade—un oficio—and there are few people, you can count them on one hand, who ever make an art of it. They say Bolden's done it and that rascal Armstrong. Emanuel Perez was a journeyman. On the piano you have Jelly Roll, but he's a pool hustler mostly. And there's Robicheaux and a couple of others.

Then Adalberto would grow pensive. He couldn't draw a deep-enough breath to blow two strong notes together, his trumpet under the bed gathering dust, his lips pursing only for the bottle. He was feeling nostalgic about Cuba, what he'd left there, what he could have been. Haunted by the specter of that truncated future, he'd suck on the bottle some more until eventually he fell asleep, sleep of the drunkard, sleep of the dead. Students knocked on the door, and he didn't answer until the next day or the day after, coming out of his drunk like a man comes back from death, disheveled and ashen, smelling like the grave itself. It got so that he'd have occasional thoughts about China in the middle of a lesson. He waved his hand in front of his face as if he were swatting flies, and the student would be dumbfounded, thinking el maestro had really lost it now. Then he'd recover and continue the lesson as if nothing had transpired.

What he had lost Adalberto found knocking at his door one day when he'd been sober for two weeks. China had put on a little weight, which made her seem less a girl and more a woman, and her mouth was not so eager to smile. Next to her was a thin, reluctant boy. He had her eyes—proud, undaunted, Chinaman's eyes. Adalberto and China looked briefly at each other; then he stepped aside and let them in.

She said she wanted lessons for the boy. He had some talent. Adalberto shook his head no, then looked out the window.

I'm booked, he lied. What happened to your man?

Passed on.

Adalberto wanted to know more but he couldn't well ask in front of the boy. The thought that Bob Rowe was dead passed quickly through his mind and he relished it.

That's his son.

I can't play anymore. Don't have the lungs. All I do now is teach, barely keep food on the table, roof over my head. That was the short version of his life. The long version wasn't worth telling.

Then you can make room for another student, China said.

Bring him around tomorrow afternoon. He turned to the boy and said, You hear that, chico? Tomorrow, four o'clock.

The light tone he used with the boy belied the misery he felt inside. That night he couldn't stop thinking of that woman, who'd nearly cost him his life, and the youthful bravado that made him think he could show up the King of the Tenderloin. At three in the morning he got up and made himself a ham sandwich, took one bite, and put it down. He pulled the case out from under the bed, opened it, and brought the instrument to his lips. He licked the mouthpiece and played a few notes, then a soft bolero he'd learned in his early days in Havana to lull the girls. The heat of the music was gone but he could still turn the notes into words, the words into notes. China. She'd turned his life into a bolero. He lay on the bed with the cornet across his chest and slept soundly for the first time in months.

Adalberto had not the heart to tell the boy or his mother that he should take up another instrument, or better yet, another trade. Secret's in the fingering, he said gently, but the boy's fingers were clumsy and lacked the delicacy to coax the valves down. Feathers, Adalberto called them. Nurse the feathers.

The lessons went on for two months, not because there was any hope of the boy getting better—you either have talent or you don't—but because the weekly visits allowed Adalberto to interact with China. He made an exception to his rule that parents should not be present during the lesson. It was too hot for her to walk back and forth, he insisted, and so she stayed, sitting in a corner of the living room while Adalberto tried his best to bring out the boy's limited ability even if he sounded like a hoarse goose in the best of moments. Adalberto's heart raced, his breath shortened, his concentration became a yellow butterfly flittering back and forth from the kitchen to the bedroom, from the bedroom to the living room. He made sure his pants were clean, his shirt pressed, and his shoes shined. Then he waited, sitting across from the window, where he could watch her come down the street and up the porch steps, pretty as ever, with that relaxed way of walking, her hips moving from side to side like a bell and black hair glistening in the hot sun. Seeing her brought back the wind he had lost, and his confidence, too, though that didn't keep him from getting nervous.

At the end of the second month she showed up without the boy. Adalberto was surprised and pleased. This time she sat on the couch, and he sat next to her after bringing her a glass of water with lime. She liked it that way.

What do you think? she said matter-of-factly.

He might be better off with another instrument, he said. The horn requires delicacy of touch. That's something you're born with—that and a good ear.

He has none of those things, she said.

Adalberto didn't contradict her. Instead he said, He's a good boy, un buen muchacho, but music's not his thing. I want to keep seeing you. He hesitated a moment, and then he added, forcing it like a bad note, I want to marry you.

China let out a loud laugh. My son's father was a pimp. I was his whore. Once a whore, always a whore.

I don't care about any of that.

You should. I've done things you don't even want to think about. Don't mess with me. There was no sadness or resignation in her voice, just a casual dismissal that unsettled Adalberto.

She left then, not letting him say another word. Adalberto spent the next three days sitting on the couch, getting up only to go to the bathroom. The whiskey bottle he'd relied on in times like these sat in the kitchen like a somber sentinel. There were knocks on the door. By then students knew to leave him alone if he didn't answer. He had visions of his sister, who'd died of typhoid fever in Havana, dancing round him like a small jaundiced angel and of his mother, who used to beat him with a broom handle when he misbehaved, and of his best friend, Lolo, who became a thief and was shot in the face by a policeman. He thought of suicide, and he thought of moving away to a place he'd never been and where no one knew him, but he lacked the will.

On the fourth day, there was another knock that sounded forceful and insistent, and for reasons he never could explain to himself, he woke from his torpor and answered the door, expecting to find there, if not the devil himself, then one of his emissaries. It was Jelly Roll, someone worse than the devil. Adalberto stood at the door like a fool, waiting for the man to say something.

He was dressed in a perfectly pressed gray suit, white shirt, solid maroon tie with a diamond pin holding it down. He was at the height of his fame then and he gave off the sweet scent of expensive cologne, the scent of success.

I know who you are, Adalberto said stepping to the side. Adalberto pointed to the couch while he sat on the old straight-backed wooden chair where he had his students sit for posture.

I heard you play that Spanish music sometime back, Jelly Roll said.

Cuban music, you mean, Adalberto said. Don't play anymore. My lungs no good.

Somebody told me about that. I first heard that music from you. I'll make it worth your while.

My while's come and gone. Lungs no good. Need a piano.

Piano I got, Jelly Roll said and insisted they go to the same club where he'd stood him up many years before.

It was the middle of the afternoon and the club was closed. Adalberto sat and played a few awkward chords. Piano was not his instrument. What he played was flat and uninspired, and Jelly Roll said to play again, up tempo, with brio. Adalberto let loose, not worrying about the mistakes he was making, and Jelly Roll poured him a tumbler of whiskey. Adalberto did his best and got out a few tunes. Jelly Roll took over and played a rag, slowing the tempo, then picking it up, moving up and down with the right while the left hand stayed in place, harmonizing with the melody, and going off on rhythmic riffs that were identical to what Adalberto used to play on his cornet, only nobody had paid attention because he was a nobody in a nobody's land.

When the session was over, Jelly Roll pulled out a roll of bills and tried to give Adalberto a hundred dollars. Adalberto refused, not out of pride. One hundred dollars more or less wasn't going to make a big difference in his life, and knowing that Jelly Roll had listened to him and learned from him and that some historian years hence would say he stole that Spanish tinge from Adalberto was satisfaction enough. He didn't need money; he needed someone to notice what he'd done back in the day.

Keep your money, Mr. Jelly Roll. I got what I wanted.

Adalberto made it home just as the sun was setting, streaks of clouds moving westward colored a vibrant orange. He was exhilarated and jumpy again, just like he got before a gig, and he wanted more than anything to play a little music, get a little sex from a sweet and sassy woman like China. Whore or no whore, she was the woman for him. He knew that the first time he saw her.

That night he went in search of her, and over the next week he scoured the city—uptown, downtown, Storyville, French Quarter. He asked dozens of people. Some had never heard of her; some had and gave him a conspiratorial smile and shake of the head. None had seen her in years, not since her man was shot at a card game. She was nowhere. He was too old for despair, but after seven full days of looking he told himself, If I can't have her, I won't have any woman.

So he went home and resumed his teaching, this time in a more relaxed manner and without the mordant criticisms he'd dole out when one of his students missed a note or lost his posture or let the horn sag down from his lips like a flower withering. Horn's your dick. Keep it up! Finally he learned what all teachers learn: You don't teach the students you want but the students you get, and he took on all comers.

Occasionally he'd go to a club, especially if one of his former students was playing—they were very insistent he go listen to them—but that club life had lost its luster, and weeks would pass without him leaving the house, except for groceries and liquor. It wasn't a bad life. He was no longer in the thrall of desire, and he could look at a beautiful woman as at a statue, admiring the beauty from a distance as he walked past, and go on about his business. By 9 PM his eyelids grew heavy, and forty-five minutes later he was in bed, covers up to his chin, even in summer, sleeping deeply through until five when his bladder woke him. Mornings were his to do with as he wished. Most of his students were schoolboys and took their lessons in the afternoon and early evening. Sometimes he did a little cleaning; mostly he sat on the front porch and watched the birds on the yard chase after bread crumbs the old, deaf landlady fed them.

He avoided thinking about the past and for the most part he was successful. Whenever the memory of his knifing came up, he stood and walked around the block looking at garden fixtures, the clouds, the trees, anything to divert his mind. New Orleans was a nice town, slow and gentle on the nerves. The past was a gray indeterminate mass that had no surface because it had no bottom. If he was going to die anywhere it would be here, a place he liked better, or remembered better, than any other. Days came and days went, interrupted by students, shy younger ones accompanied by their mothers and cocky older ones on their own. Without knowing it, Adalberto had become a fixture like a church or a barbershop. El maestro. That pleased him most of all.

All ambition left him. He didn't care if he was the best teacher in town or the worst, the richest or the poorest. Some men liked to collect women, and some men liked to eat and drink well, but he was not driven in those directions. People knew him, took him for granted even, and he didn't mind that, nor did he mind that slowly, imperceptibly, those people died and younger ones took their place who didn't recognize him on the street and therefore were not compelled to engage him in conversation, chat about the weather or the house falling down at the corner or the runaway dog that had bitten one of the children on the next block. Then one day when he was shaving, he looked at himself in the mirror and saw a man, older-looking than his years, but glowing with contentment, who went to bed at night and got up in the morning because he couldn't imagine doing anything else. He had no wife to care for, no children to feed. His students' faces, and those of their mothers, were as blank and indistinguishable as he was to them. El maestro. That he'd once had a past and that the future was coming at him faster than he could figure didn't matter. At a moment's notice he could be gone and forgotten, less than a blip in people's memory, replaced by a younger, more dynamic teacher who would know the latest techniques, the newest sounds.

What's the hottest music? one of his students repeated, incredulous, when Adalberto asked. Jazz, man, jazz.

Jazz, Adalberto said. That's not new.

The way Jelly Roll plays it, nobody's ever done before. The left hand does crazy things, improvises on the rhythm so the piano sounds like a drum.

As it should, Adalberto said. Piano's a percussion instrument.

But the rhythm's not regular. It varies and the melody moves off the rhythm.

The clave beat from the habanera. Cubans been doing that for a while, moving off the six/eight on the downbeat, then back again.

Jelly Roll calls it Spanish tinge.

My ass, Adalberto said with a smirk. It ain't Spanish. It's Cuban.

Spanish, Cuban, what's the difference? the young man said. He was barely out of his teens, thought he was Columbus discovering the world.

Look at me, buster. You think they have people with my color skin in Spain?

You could be Creole, the young man said.

I am criollo, bobera. I got African blood and I got Spanish. I'm Cuban and so's those rhythms. He heard them from me first. I was playing at the St. George with a band full of nobodies and Jelly Roll comes in a few times. Then he disappears. Goes up north to Chicago, L.A. Now's he's calling it the Spanish tinge and I'm still a nobody without lungs.

Adalberto sent the young musician away without a lesson and thought maybe he'd reached the end of his teaching. Jelly Roll was out there in the world making music, and a new generation was gaining on him strong. Music was changing and he didn't know what it was changing into. He stepped out to the store to buy himself some cigarettes, mull the thing over. On his way he walked past a blooming magnolia under which lay an old bicycle. The bicycle, rusted and mangled, was covered with petals fallen from the tree. There now, that's a good way to go, broken, covered with flowers. And this thought was followed almost immediately by the fact that he was only forty. Strange to think his life was over. There's any number of things he could do. He could be a bartender or a club manager; he could open up a music store or become a housepainter. Lots of houses in New Orleans needed paint.

Involved in these thoughts, he opened the door to the store, and just as he entered a gust of wind hit him square on the face. It was a sweet-smelling kind of wind, perfumed with gardenias and moist, as if it had come off the ocean. It had none of that grocery-store smell—stale carton and pickles and salt bacon all mixed together. Jackson, the owner, sat behind the counter chewing on a toothpick and drinking out of a coffee cup. The store was as Adalberto had always known it—several rows of canned goods and, up along the far wall, sacks of rice and dry beans of various kinds. Something, though, was different, and not just the smell. He nodded to Jackson and Jackson nodded back and asked what he wanted. Adalberto didn't answer.

Instead he walked the length of the establishment, looking down each row until he reached the last, which he followed to the end with the line of his sight. There she was, leaning over a sack, shoveling red beans into a paper bag. He had a strong desire to call her name, but every time he tried, no sound came out of his mouth. He felt nauseated and tasted the bitter bile from long ago in his mouth, the knife going into him, the pain, the deflation. There she was, China, and he couldn't even say her name. He heard a voice urging him to go to her and another telling him to stay away. A powerful struggle went on inside him between what he'd wanted and what he'd lost, the forces of ambition and love and the forces of defeat. The store tilted and he almost fell over sideways to the wooden floor, but he grabbed hold of a post and leaned against it, taking deep breaths until the world was level again.

He made his decision, which was based neither on reason nor on passion but on a reluctance to give up any more of his life than he had. He retraced his steps back to the front of the store and slipped out the door. It was spring and the sun was out and trees were blooming all over the neighborhood. He walked home without the cigarettes, taking his time, past the broken bicycle and the magnolia tree, past the old houses and the ones just recently built. He didn't know what year it was—1928, 1938? He sat on the porch a long while, not moving much. No one came in or out, not his fellow tenants or his landlady or the postman. The birds had flown away looking for food in another yard. He was stuck, somewhere between the living and the dead, the soft afternoon sun making everything creamy. It was a great day to be alive, someone might have said a block or two away. He sat until the shadows lengthened and the day turned to night and the night into an open space that could only be measured by the depth and breadth of all he was and ever would be.

STORYTELLER

I had just finished bathing Papa and was applying liniment on his chest when he said something very soft, which sounded like radio static. As I bent over and asked him to repeat it, he arched his back, let out a long moan, and didn't take another breath. I sat on the bed, unsure what to do, call the police, an ambulance, a priest? What would they say about Mama, mummified next to him? Why hadn't I called after she died? There are laws, you know. What story could I possibly tell? She tried to kill me.

A flock of creatures swept through the bedroom window. They flew around me in tight swooping turns, grazing my face with their wings and pecking at my ears. At first I thought they were demons coming to fetch Papa's soul. They were smaller than I imagined, and from them emanated a sweet odor of tenderness and severity, not the stench of sulfur. They weren't demons but angels come to take him to a different place. The peace they had experienced through eternity made them impervious to any kind of human suffering. All I could feel was the relief of someone liberated at last from the chains of obligation. Everything's a story, I tell you.

Angels on the dresser, cooing and pecking the warped wood; angels on the bed, ministering to Papa with divine ablutions, chanting in all the languages that have ever existed, as well as a few that had not yet been created. I stood away, arms over my head, until they were finished with their rites and had flown back to their perches. I made my way toward Papa and felt for his body, which had acquired the texture of melted cheese. It was too soon for decomposition and I couldn't figure out what they had done to him, what interstellar acids they had bathed him in. I lowered my hand to his belly again, gathered some of the curdly substance, and brought it to my nose. It was like nothing I'd smelled before, seawater and milk and roasted poppy seeds and toilet-tank water. My mind went in circles around the smell, trying to identify it. I stuck out my tongue and tasted, and I knew it was bird shit Papa was covered in, not angelic fluids. I screamed at the angels; I swatted at them as they flew by inside the room, beating the air with their wings, cooing maniacally. They bounced against the walls and ceiling until they found the window and flew out flapping, leaving behind a faint avian scent and a rain of downy feathers that stuck to my head and arms and gathered on the floor.

I cried a long while. I'd never felt such desolation. I was smeared in shit and feathers. I was blind. I knew nothing of the world outside the door, how to make my way into it, how to survive within it, and I had no one to pity me but myself. Some liberation.

Then the trumpet sounded outside, the one I heard when Mama died, playing a tune as softly as a horn can play. I lay by the bed listening, a cool breeze accompanying the music, bringing the promise of warm weather. It was a song called "Ausencia," Mama's favorite, which she sang to me on a day when she was breathing well enough to feel nostalgic. It told of birds returning to the nest and of other birds who love and leave and never come back. I'd had enough of birds. You know how song lyrics are. They never make sense when you need them to. I left the bedroom. I heard the click of the bedroom door behind me and I walked quietly away. In the living room the horn was muffled, almost inaudible. I couldn't stay in the apartment. The world had many doors to pass through.

In the lobby I heard the super calling after me, asking if there was anything he could get me. I knew where I was going. On the street I could hear the music clearly again. I followed the tune as if I were reeling in the big fish, the one I'd so wanted to catch all the time by the river, pole in hand, head in the clouds, eyes on the waters of my imagining. I went down the street to the corner and waited for someone to help me cross. Cars swished by me and trucks with their murderous engines. There were sirens and horns, drunks and derelicts, men and women passing by, invisible, unknowable. A taxi stopped, thinking I needed a ride. Beyond the river of traffic was the horn player, blaring out his tune. I sensed someone next to me waiting for the light to change. I was afraid to ask for help, thinking I'd

PABLO MEDINA

be discovered, rebuffed, sent back where I belonged. I fought myself hard, as one fights the counteraction of a fish trying to throw the hook.

Could you tell me when the light is green? I asked, sounding timid and slow minded, the king's English lurking just under each word.

Wassat? he said in Cubop City speech, no breath wasted.

I'm blind, I said.

Where's your stick?

I don't have one.

Light's green, the man said.

I expected him to grab my arm and help me across but he was already gone. I put my arms out and stepped off the curb, following the taut line of sound. I must have appeared like a sleepwalker or a zombie to the drivers. I could feel the heat of their motors, the glow of their metal. When I reached the other side of the street, I tripped on the curb and fell against a newspaper box. I lay on the sidewalk struggling to get up as people walked past me. I could hear them chattering, their soles slapping the sidewalk. I took a deep breath and got myself up with the aid of the box and kept going, still with arms outstretched until I was right in front of the music man.

Hey, music man, where are you from? I thought nothing of asking.

The playing stopped. I was at the edge of the world, about to fall off.

I'm Rican. What of it?

At that moment I knew I'd caught the big fish, the one I hoped to bring my parents in their sickness. There was no way I was going back to the apartment now.

You were playing my mother's favorite song.

Oh yea? She a romantic woman?

She's dead.

Sorry about that, Papo. We all gotta go sometime. Listen, I'm wondering if you could help me out and count the money that's in the case, you know? I'm blind and I can't see if I got five cents or fifty dollars in there.

I was about to move toward the music man and I let out a laugh. It was more like a whinny.

Whoa there, he said. What's so funny?

I'm blind, too, I said.

That's a coincidence, the music man said.

Well, almost. I can see a little. I have to get very close to see what's in your case.

Do it. We might have enough in there for a couple of beers.

I did as I was told. Anywhere else people would be wondering what that man was doing looking into the blind man's horn case. Stealing his money? Hey you, get away from that poor blind man. Might even throw a karate kick in my direction. But here in Cubop City? I could be strangling the blind man and no one would care. Blow that horn and let it happen. Nothing personal.

Nineteen dollars and seventy-three cents.

That'll buy us a few.

The music man packed his horn. He got his stick and stood. He told me to grab his arm and I did.

Hey, Papo, he said, you smell terrible. Where you been?

Hiding, I said.

I got a shower in my place. My woman's blind, too, but she can smell a rat's asshole a mile away. Vente, Papo. We'll clean you up.

I didn't respond but let the Puerto Rican lead me to the subway entrance at the corner. We stood at the top of the stairs a moment, grabbed the handrail, and descended into the underworld.

ACKNOWLEDGMENTS

Earlier versions of parts of this book originally appeared in the following publications: *Cerise Press, Havana Noir, Las Vegas Noir, The Normal School, Shaking Like a Mountain, Switchback,* and *Water-Stone Review.*

This book would not exist in its present form without the intelligent and careful editorial suggestions of Elisabeth Schmitz, my editor at Grove/Atlantic, her associate, Jessica Monahan, and Michael Hornburg, managing editor; Mark Statman and Rufi Cole, who read the manuscript and offered valuable advice; and my agent, Elaine Markson, whose encouragement, support, and friendship over the years has been invaluable.

My son, Pablo A., has acted in his usual capacity as sounding board and tuning fork. I show him everything I write. Arístides Falcón Paradí provided much of the information about

Cuban music and folklore. My colleagues at the University of Nevada, Las Vegas, and Emerson College in Boston, offered me their trust and friendship. Without them I would be bereft. I also wish to thank Dylan Everdell and Heather Fabrizzi, for their island hospitality and warmth.